The Influencers

SHAWN MIHALIK

Asymmetrical Press

Published by Asymmetrical Press.

This book is a work of fiction. Any resemblance to persons living or dead is coincidental.

Library of Congress Cataloging-In-Publication Data
The influencers / Shawn Mihalik — 1st ed.
ISBN: 978-1-68287-026-6
eISBN: 978-1-68287-027-3
WC: 47,785
1. Social Media. 2. Los Angeles. 3. Celebrities. 4. Academy Awards. 5. Thrillers.

Cover design by Shawn Mihalik
Typeset in Garamond
Formatted in beautiful Central Oregon
Printed in the U.S.A.

Author info:
Website: www.ShawnMihalik.com
Twitter: @ShawnMihalik

ASYM METR ICAL

For Aadrial

"I don't know," he said. "Just driving."
"But this road doesn't go anywhere," I told him.
"That doesn't matter."
"What does?" I asked, after a little while.
"Just that we're on it, dude."

— Bret Easton Ellis, *Less Than Zero*

The Influencers

KENNEDY

"Everything I've ever done has been an attempt to connect with other people on a deeper level"—is what I tell Beckett after he returns to the bedroom with two white mugs of black coffee.

"Or," he says, handing me a mug, not sliding into bed next to me but remaining standing, "each action you've taken has been motivated by pure selfishness, by a forever unsated hunger for the world to know your name."

I consider this. I take a sip of the coffee. I nod. I tell Beckett he very well could be right.

Beckett saunters into the bathroom and I hear the hollow clink of his mug being set on the counter. I hear a less hollow clunk of the toilet seat being raised. I hear Beckett propel a stream of piss into the bowl.

"So what are your plans for the day?" he calls to me over the tinkle of urine striking porcelain.

"Well isn't that kind of fucking obvious?" I reply.

He comes out of the bathroom, mug back in his hands. He did not wash them. He has a habit of, after urinating, wiping his hands on a towel but not actually running them under water or applying soap. I think about this each time I'm in his bathroom and move to use his hand towel to dry my face. Sometimes I catch myself before the cloth touches my skin. Sometimes I don't, and I know it's no different from having Beckett inside of me.

"Of course it's obvious," he says with some scorn. "But I mean *before* that. What are you doing this morning? What are you doing this afternoon? When do you have to start getting ready? Is getting ready like an all-day thing? Are you going to smoke? Are you going to drink? Or will you show up for the whole thing stone-cold sober."

Beckett knows I don't touch substances. He's known this for the six months we've been together. He sometimes tells me it's stupid I don't touch them, especially pot, since I'm always advocating for its legalization and all. I argue that just because I'm for the legalization of marijuana doesn't mean I think it's good for you, or that I've done marijuana before, a lot. I don't tell him that I'm not actually for the legalization of marijuana, that I just pretend to be because advocating for the legalization of soft drugs is pretty much a prerequisite of left-wing activism. In reality I just don't have an opinion at all.

"I'm going sober," I say.

Beckett scoffs. "Well I damn well couldn't."

"Good thing you're not going then."

"Yeah, fucking good thing. I don't *want* to go anyway—I've already told you that."

"Like a dozen times."

"Well I don't."

"You're not," I say.

Beckett is mad because he wasn't invited to attend the Oscars. Of course he wasn't invited to attend—what has Beckett ever done? I'm going because I had two small roles last year in indie films. Good for you, Beckett says whenever I bring it up. I try to tell him it's not really a big deal. One of the films is up for Best Picture, and the other for Best Adapted Screenplay, but the screenplay one has nothing to do with me because I'm not a writer, and the best picture one I barely have anything to do with because my role was, like, so so small. Seriously, I was on screen for one and a half minutes. I had two lines.

"Two lines during which you conversed with George Clooney," Beckett says derisively. Every time he says the name *George Clooney* he sucks his cheeks in and swallows. Like he's salivating. Like either he's drooling or wants to spit in Clooney's face—I can't tell which. But he swallows. I don't know whether Beckett is jealous because I'm going to the Oscars, because I have nicer followers than him, because I met George Clooney, or because, in the movie, George's character was trying to fuck me—but I do know he's jealous. It's obvious. I'm pretty intuitive—I'm a Scorpio—and I can tell he's jealous.

"Fuck the Oscars," Beckett says now. And under his breath, into his mug: "Fuck George Clooney." But, again, I can't tell whether he hates Clooney or actually wants to fuck him.

I roll onto my side, facing Beckett more directly. My right tit spills out from Beckett's beige sheet. I don't pull the sheet back over it. "Anyway, I have to go back to my flat this morning and get a few things. Then I have a meeting at nine with J-Sean Laurentius. Did I tell you Arnold somehow got him to design my dress? I guess they have to make sure all the measurements are still good, in case I, like, got fat or something in the last few weeks. Then I have some other things to do. Then back to J-Sean to actually put the dress on —apparently it's going to take like a whole team of people, like three or four people, I haven't actually seen the dress yet but Arnold says it's brilliant—and then Arnold's sending a limo."

Beckett's phone dings and he pulls it from somewhere and is checking it. I don't know where he could have pulled it from. He's wearing only boxer briefs. His skin is very tan. His abs are smooth. His pecs are large. He makes a scrolling motion with his thumb. "I hate when you use that word," he says.

"What word?" I ask, even though I know what word.

"Flat," he says.

I've used the world "flat" instead of "apartment" ever since my trip to Europe last year. It's a better word. I like it more. Beckett says it sounds posh, tells me it makes me sound fake. Maybe that's why I use it: because I like sounding posh or because I know it annoys Beckett. And, anyway, how can I be fake for doing the things I do if they are, after all, the things I do—if *I'm* doing them?

"Anything interesting going on there?" I ask.

"Hmmm?"

"Anything interesting going on on your phone."

"Oh—not really," he says. "Just some notifications."

"Right," I say. I realize I haven't checked mine yet this morning. I grab my phone from the bedside table.

"So you were saying—" Beckett says.

I look at him. "What?"

"You were telling me about your dream. Something about being deep with other people . . ."

"Oh, yeah," I say.

KENNEDY

There is nothing interesting waiting for me on my phone, but I scroll for several minutes anyway. I have a text message from Arnold reminding me of my meeting with J-Sean Laurentius at nine— which is annoying, the reminder, because of course I put the meeting in my calendar and so another one of my notifications is a reminder from the calendar of the meeting with J-Sean at nine. Arnold knows I put things on my calendar—I even shared the calendar with him, although I don't think he ever accepted the invitation—but still he always texts me. Every single time. I think he has his *own* calendar with my name on it that he puts all my events he's scheduled for me on. Probably does that with each of his clients. Which makes sense. That's what agents do.

I have email notifications turned on but I don't actually ever check my email. I don't know anyone my age who checks their email—not actors, anyway. Maybe there are some techie types I know who do. I think about this one guy I know, Brock, and his office chat startup. I'm sure Brock's used email, but does he actually use it now? I doubt it. That would be hypocritical. Then it occurs to me that Nancy uses email.

Because I always get email from her, like about protest marches she's organizing and stuff. But I never respond. I just show up at the marches so I can get some photos of me at them. This morning I have an email notification that my next visit to Marty's Coffee is my 50th, so here's a coupon for 50 percent off to celebrate. There's also a notification that I haven't been to Trickling Brook Coffee since that one time a few days after it opened, and they miss me, so here's a coupon for 25 percent off, they'd love to see me some time.

I go to Marty's Coffee so much because I like their very white aesthetic. Like the paint, I mean. I don't mean anything racist or race-related. Marty is Philippino. Or at least one of the baristas their is. I don't actually know whether it's Marty, or whether Marty is even real. But there's this barista who I see most of the times I'm in there. I assume he's Marty. Someone from Marty's Coffee pays Arnold, and then Arnold pays me, and in exchange I go to Marty's Coffee once a week or so and post a photo. The white aesthetic makes the place perfect for photos. Arnold tried to work out an arrangement with Trickling Brook, but they didn't have the budget. Maybe they do now, now that they've been open a while.

I tell Siri to remind me to ask Arnold to check back with Trickling Brook about whether they have the budget.

I don't open the email notifications. Somehow they just eventually disappear from my screen.

There's a Yelp notification to try a new coffee shop near me: Pinewood Coffee and Tea. I tell Siri to remind me about this, too.

I don't have Instagram notifications turned on. I used to, but once I hit 10,000 followers I just had to turn them off. And now I have . . . 40 times that? Notifications would drive me insane.

But I do open Instagram and scroll through for a few minutes and like some stuff. I'm not really paying attention. I'm thinking about how I get to go to the Oscars tonight. How technically I could win an Oscar for Best Picture. I tap the little heart in the bottom (I have thousands of likes and comments since yesterday) and start liking some comments on my posts. If *In My Eyes, Your Heart* does win Best Picture, I won't actually get to go up with the rest of the cast and crew to accept it. My part was way too small for that. But I'll get to watch George Clooney and the director and everyone get up there and know that I was a part of what they're up there for.

"You know," Arnold told me the other day, "if the movie wins Best Picture, in a way, part of that award is mine, too, because I found you the part."

I don't think that's how it works, but I didn't tell him that. Arnold's never had a client who was nominated for an award before. I know how much it means to him.

"You know—" I say to Beckett. But then I realize he's in the shower. I request an Uber. I put my shirt on and grab my bag from the living room and slip my shoes on by the door and head downstairs.

ARNOLD

Kennedy Thorne hasn't responded to my text about her meeting this morning with J-Sean Laurentius and to be honest it's really stressing me out. I try to drink my orange juice but my eyes keep drifting to my phone, which is on the table, face up. I'm waiting for the screen to light up with a response from Kennedy. Sometimes the screen does light up but it's not Kennedy. It's someone else or something else.

"Put that away, Arnold," Esmeralda says. I call her Ismi, because when we were first dating, for like five months I thought her name was Ismeralda for some reason, with an I. I still think Ismeralda is a prettier name than Esmeralda.

"I can't just put it away," I reply. "Today is a very big day. Today is a huge huge day and—"

"And if Kennedy messes it up it's going to look bad on you and no one will ever work with you again. I know. I know you think that, but I don't think that's true. You have a dozen other clients—"

"None of my other clients are winning Oscars today, Ismi. And it's not clients I'm worried about. I'm worried *for* my clients. Do you know how hard it was to get J-Sean Laurentius to design a dress for a woman who basically does nothing but show up in other people's YouTube videos and talk about what a disaster the president is?"

"I would think talking about what a disaster the president is would be a prerequisite for working with someone like J-Sean Laurentius. Isn't that a prerequisite for doing just about anything in this town?"

"No. No—he doesn't care about politics. He's a fashion designer."

"Fashion designers are artists, Arnold."

"Yes, but they're not *that* kind of artist, like not the regular kind. Laurentius just cares about clothes and…and blowjobs."

"That's sexist, Arnold."

"It's not sexist. The word you're thinking of is homophobic. But it's not that either. Blowjobs are fine. Nobody cares if you give blowjobs."

Ismi harrumphs. Probably because *she* doesn't give blowjobs. At least not for the last 22 years. That's how long we've been married. My first wife gave me lots of blowjobs.

My phone lights up. I lean over to look at the screen. It's not Kennedy. It's Penny Isaacson. I sigh.

"She's a kid, Arnold. She's probably not even up yet."

I look at my watch. I could look at my phone but I look at my watch. "She *should* be. If she's not, she's lazy."

I take a sip of my orange juice. I pat my breast pocket, trying to find my statins. I can feel the steady increase of my blood pressure.

"You left them on the kitchen counter."

"Are you sure?"

"I saw them there myself, on our way out the door."

"Fuck," I say. "Why didn't you say anything? Fuck." I suppose I could hop around the corner and grab them. Ismi and I eat breakfast at this cafe most mornings because it's a three-minute walk from our house. We still live in Larchmont Village. It's not like any of my clients are A-listers, but I've done okay.

As I debate walking back to the house, I see the waiter coming over with my plate of French toast and I know I'll probably forget to take my statins today. My screen lights up again. It's just the same message from Penny Isaacson. I get double notifications for every text message if I don't check it after the first one. I don't like this feature but I don't know how to turn it off.

"This looks delicious," Ismi says.

I love Ismi. I've loved her for more than 22 years. But right now I kind of hate her—just in this moment, just for a second. Because she *knows* the French toast is going to be delicious. She eats it almost every day. I eat it almost every day. My doctor told me I should switch to egg whites, so I try to eat egg whites on Sundays when we have breakfast at home before church, but I'm always hungry after.

Fuck, I'm always hungry after French toast, too.

"Can you pass the syrup, dear?" Ismi says.

I pour syrup on my own French toast and then hand it over to her.

When I first took on Penny Isaacson as a client I told her she should change her last name to something with a better ring to it. Turned out she *had* changed her last name to something with a better ring to it: Isaacson. Her real last name was Squelch. And you're set on *Isaacson*? I asked her. She was. God knows why.

I take a bite of my French toast. There's not enough syrup, but knowing what my doctor would say, I don't add more. I pick up my phone and open Penny's text message and start to type a reply to her.

"Is it her?" Ismi asks.

"No," I say. "It's just Penny fucking Isaacson. Asking whether I got her tickets to the Philharmonic for Friday."

"Oh. Did you?"

"I'm working on it! There's this Russian tenor flying in to do a performance with them or something and apparently he's a big deal and it's all sold out."

"Why does she want to go to the symphony anyway? Isn't she like 25?"

"She just wants to be able to post about it on her Instagram. Nobody likes the symphony, but it's some weird thing where if you're young and you go and you post about it everybody thinks you're sophisticated."

"Well, somebody must like it."

I stop texting. "What?"

"Somebody must like the symphony. If it's sold out."

I roll my eyes and resume texting. I tell Penny Isaacson not to get her hopes up.

"Your food is getting cold, dear."

I sigh. I put my phone down. Then I say, "One last thing" and pick it up again and send Kennedy Thorne one more message reminding her that she has to meet J-Sean. I put it down again. If she doesn't respond I'm just going to choose to assume she made it to the fitting.

"Put it in your pocket," Ismi says.

I sigh again. Fine. I put the phone in my pocket. Just after I do I feel it buzz but my hand is already on my fork and I think, *Fuck it, I'm going to enjoy my breakfast.* I haven't enjoyed my breakfast in 22 years.

"You should take some CBD when you get home," Ismi says. "You're too stressed."

"Actually," I say, "I think I saw CBD coffee on the menu. I'll just order one of those."

"You're not supposed to drink coffee."

I signal for the waiter. "I think the CBD makes it okay."

BECKETT

I stay in the shower a little longer than normal because I hope Kennedy will take a hint and leave while I'm in here. I actually really like Kennedy—at least I like her as much as anyone else I'm fucking, probably more, and if it happens that she's the last person I got to fuck in this world, that's all right with me. I mean, she's enthusiastic and her pussy is shaved and she's not shy about spit when she deep throats—but I just have a lot on my mind this morning, and I can't have her be a part of it. For her sake.

I think I hear the bedroom door close, and then maybe even the front door, but with the water running I doubt I could actually hear those sounds, so I'm probably imagining them, thinking wishfully. Despite everything going on today, everything weighing on my mind, the anxiety, the near-paralyzing fear, my dick starts to get hard and I consider jacking off, which will keep me in the shower even longer. But the thing is I can't stay in the shower *too* long. I have places to be. I'll just have to get out at some point and if Kennedy is still here I'll just have to tell her, respectfully, that I'm sorry but I have to split. Besides—the instant I start thinking about jacking off my dick goes all soft again, which is probably for the best.

I turn off the water and grab a towel and open the bathroom door and, so that she doesn't *feel* like I'm trying to kick her out, say loudly, "Hey, so I'd love to get breakfast or something but—"

The bedroom is empty. I head into the living room and the rest of the apartment is empty too. My apartment is quite small. Like 600 square feet and it still costs me a couple grand a month. But at least it's easy to tell there's no one here.

I go back to the bedroom. Kennedy's coffee mug is on my nightstand and I can see she drank maybe a sip from it. I'm kind of annoyed she left it there. She could at least have put it on the counter in the kitchen. I can feel something churning in my solar plexus. My towel falls to the floor. I've never been able to figure out how to tie a towel so that it stays around my waist even though my waist is only 28 inches and I have these big oversized fluffy towels I bought at Crate and Barrel. I breathe the way my therapist taught me. Slowly. One two three four five. One two three four five. The churning in my solar plexus settles down. The thing that was churning is still there, has been my whole life, but I don't give in to it this morning. Later—I can give in to it later. That's what today is all about.

"Alexa," I say, "play something that's good for ending your life to."

"I can't find a song called 'Something That's Good for Ending Your Life To,'" Alexa says.

Whatever. "Play something energetic. I don't know— something by Drake or Cardi B."

"Playing Prince Radio."

Whatever. I've never listened to Prince on this device before, so I don't know what Alexa is thinking, but I allow it. I heard somewhere that Prince was a Jehovah's Witness. I heard that Donald Glover was a Jehovah's Witness. I change my mind. "Alexa, play Childish Gambino."

Alexa either doesn't hear me or ignores me. "Little Red Corvette" keeps playing. Whatever.

I debate whether I should eat breakfast or fast till lunch or fast all day and never eat another meal again, maybe just slit my wrists right now. I've been intermittent fasting for like six months now. Combined with this new ketogenic diet I'm on and the CrossFit box I go to, I've got pretty killer abs. I throw on a brown polo and then decide brown looks stupid and I should never wear brown, so I switch into a blue polo. I find my jeans on the floor where I left them last night and pull them on. I head back into the living room and fill a large glass with water and add some oil of oregano, for immune protection and gut health, and as I'm drinking it I start to laugh.

KENNEDY

My Uber driver's name is Carlos and he pulls up in an off-white Ford Fusion. The app says he'll be driving a *white* Ford Fusion, so I'm a little skeptical. I know it sounds silly, the difference between white and off-white, but you wouldn't believe how many creepy Uber drivers I've had. Or maybe you would. I've heard there are a lot of creepy Uber drivers. My friend Penny Isaacson says an Uber driver tried to kiss her once. When she told me, I laughed and said are you sure it wasn't Travis Kalanick. Who? she said. The CEO of Uber, I tried to tell her, but she just stared at me blankly. Penny's a sweet girl, but she's kind of a dumb cunt, too, and doesn't ever really read the news or keep up with current events. The porn star Jenny St. Star posted on Instagram and Twitter a couple months ago that her Uber driver had insisted she sit in the front seat and then when she did he tried to slide his hand up her skirt. She tried to get out but the door was locked, she said. Supposedly the driver in question was fired, according to Uber, but of course that's not enough, and Jenny occasionally posts updates about ongoing litigation that doesn't seem to be going anywhere. I met Jenny St. Star at a pool party last summer and she seemed like a nice girl—she seemed smart, with a good business head on her shoulders.

I should probably delete Uber from my phone and switch to Lyft, but setting up a new account takes time. And anyway, off-white and white aren't *that* different. I squint so that I can see through the tinted windows as the car pulls up, trying not to seem obvious as I do so.

"Kennedy?" Carlos asks as I slide into the back seat.

"That's me."

"Great! Beautiful morning, isn't it? Where we heading?"

Uber drivers always ask that. Then they always answer their own question—

"Dorrington? In West Hollywood West?" he asks, looking at his phone, which is mounted on the dashboard. "Does that sound right?"

"That's what I typed into the app."

"Great! Off we go!"

It's only a 10-minute drive from Beckett's flat to mine. If the drive were any longer, I wouldn't have stayed at his place last night, not with everything I have going on today. I'd be lying if I said I wasn't nervous about tonight, or even about meeting J-Sean Laurentius, but I'm not really nervous. In the last few years, I've become more and more used to doing things like meeting famous people. I mean, I did get to flirt with George Clooney. Sure, it's because we were enacting lines from a script, but that's pretty significant too: I was in a movie, with George Clooney, in the same scene, and we had lines directed at each other.

Well—*he* had lines directed at *me*. My character hardly talked. She just kind of stood there sheepishly while Clooney flirted with her. And then she giggled, handed him a key, and told him his room number. It's weird that that was a year and a half ago. Movie production takes longer than I realized. It's not like YouTube, where you go over to the Creator's studio, which is usually this corner of their living room or their kitchen that's been cleaned up real nice, and stand in front of a camera and BS while making cocktails or while drinking cocktails and cooking something, and then they edit and upload the thing like a day later.

I put everything I had into that giggle.

Carlos the Uber driver says, "Did you get up to anything fun last night?"

"Excuse me?" I say. I can't believe he just asked that.

"I'm sorry?" he says. "I didn't mean to offend you or anything. It's just L.A., you know? Saturday night. Everyone's always up to something. Parties and whatnot."

I want to ask him what business it is of his who I slept with last night, but I know that's probably not what he's asking. You can request a quiet Uber ride these days, but like an uncaffeinated idiot I didn't think to select that option. It shouldn't even *be* an option you have to select. "Quiet Uber ride" should be the default. You should be able to, if you want, choose a talkative driver, like if you're a lonely person or something.

"I was at a fundraiser," I tell him. "For this guy who's running for Congress."

"Ah," Carlos says. "I'm not very political. I'm not technically a citizen yet, but when I am, I don't know if I'm going to vote, you know? It doesn't seem worth it. Like no matter what I do—who I vote for, I mean—someone's going to criticize me for it."

The truth is I don't really care about politics either, but back during the 2016 election when I said something about Trump on my Instagram Story—I think Stories had just come out and suddenly everyone stopped using Snapchat—something about him being a "buffoon" or something, which is not a word I'd normally use, but I'd heard my day say it so I just kind of repeated it into the camera, it found its way onto Buzzfeed. Something like "Popular Instagram Comedian Speaks Out Against Trump." It wasn't like I was doing anything new. Everyone was speaking out against Trump. I wasn't even a "popular comedian," not yet. I had maybe 100k followers. I was doing these less-than-60-second videos recorded on my phone. My college boyfriend Ricky was the one writing them. I just put on a wig and did what he told me to. But then, after I called Trump a buffoon, I guess I was expected to be an activist, whatever that means. I'm honestly not sure what happened next because I was pretty fucked up for like three months—not on anything hard, just this phase where I was smoking a lot of pot every day with Ricky—but not long after, we broke up and I dropped out of college and moved to California. Somewhere in there I got to 400k followers.

"You don't have to tell people who you voted for," I say to Carlos. "They have no right to ask, either."

"They just look at me and assume, though," he says. "Like, because my English is good and my accent isn't very strong, they think I'm already a citizen and assume I voted for Hillary."

"*Would* you have voted for Hillary?" I can't help but ask. I pinch my leg discretely because all I want to do is scroll through my feed and respond to comments. That's what you *do* during Uber rides.

"I mean, I don't know. All that stuff about her emails. . . . I don't think I trust her, man."

"Mmmhmm," I can't help but say.

"And then it's like, if they don't assume I voted for Hillary, then they assume I'm here illegally, which is just . . . neither of those things are fucking true, y'know."

"Mmmhmm," I say again, but this time with more control.

"Anyway—did you know I'm not just an Uber driver?"

"You don't say," I say.

"Oh no—I'm an actor."

"Ah," I say.

"It's why I moved here."

"To America."

"To *Los Angeles*. I moved to America to be a doctor. I got this foreign aid scholarship thing to U.C. Santa Barbara. Be a doctor, my dad said. He helped me figure the whole thing out. I got the scholarship, because my grades were so high, and I was going to be a cardiologist—"

"Like your dad?"

"What? Oh, no—my dad's a bricklayer in Tijuana."

"Oh."

"He was real proud of me though."

"That's good."

"Yeah—until I dropped out. Says I'm wasting my potential. Says I'm gonna get deported now."

"I . . . dropped out too." I don't know why my mouth keeps talking. I pull my phone out to signal some sort of end to the conversation. I swipe up and it unlocks when it sees my face.

"See! You *get it!* You have to do what you have to do."

I am deliberate. I don't respond this time. I open Instagram.

"But now my dad says I'm gonna get deported 'cause I'm not in school. Says school was the only thing giving me a path into this country. But I saw that movie *Coco*, you know—I love Pixar—and it was just like, so true to my culture, and I was like that kid, but I wanted to be an actor, not a musician, and I said, fuck it, fuck you dad, and dropped out and moved here. And like, I had this one tense thing with an ICE agent in a 7-Eleven once, but because I have almost no accent it hasn't really been a problem. My dad won't talk to me, though. Except on Sundays. He still always calls me on Sundays to see how I'm doing. Life is fucking hard, man, you know?"

"Mmmhmm," I say.

"Fuck, man. But you gotta do what you gotta do to follow your dreams."

I have over 1000 comments on my photo from yesterday evening at the fundraiser. I got a picture with the congressman, or potential congressman. I honestly can't remember whether he's running for election or *re*election. I just go to these things because Arnold tells me to. He knows the activist thing works out so well for me, so he makes sure I keep it up. He's got some guy who writes the captions for whenever it's time for me to post something political. Or maybe he writes them—I don't know. The congressman is kind of old, but whatever. He pinched my butt, I could have sworn, as we were taking photos. Or, I don't know, maybe he didn't. I was a little high. Then I met Beckett for dinner at Smokey Joe's, which is actually a pretty upscale place, despite the name, which is the joke, I guess.

"Anyway, Saturday night in L.A., am I right? I actually got pretty fucked up myself, once my Uber shift was over. Fuuuuck. I'm actually, like, so hung over right now. But I downed three Red Bulls and got in the car because I need to make that money. So, anyway, yeah, what do you do?"

I'm responding to comments—just liking most of them, but responding to a few—and I've finally managed to tune the Uber driver out. I try to make myself even forget his name. But I'm a people person at heart, so I still know it's Carlos. "I'm a . . . secretary," I tell him for some reason. Can't tell him I'm an actor. You don't want to tell aspiring actors that you've actually been in movies. I've never actually done that, so I don't know what would happen, but I have this intuition that it's not something you want to do.

"Oh," Carlos says. "Anyway—we're here."

I look up and he's right. We're outside my building. "Thanks," I tell him.

Outside on the curb I take a moment to give him five stars and a $3 tip.

"Morning, Ms. Thorne," the desk clerk says when I enter the lobby. I immediately wish I'd taken the side entrance. "Package for you," he says. The desk clerk is a thirty-something attractive black man, although his hair is going gray prematurely. I can never remember his name, and I feel bad about that. He's asked me out for drinks before, but I always make up some excuse. He's an aspiring actor, too. I know he follows me on Instagram.

"Good morning," I say, smiling.

"Package for you." He hands me a square box, about a foot by a foot. I haven't ordered anything lately, and there are no Amazon labels on it, so I know it must be from a sponsor or potential sponsor. Sponsorships go through Arnold. I remember when I had to do them myself. That was a lot of work. I'm glad I don't have to handle them anymore.

I use the security fob on my keychain to call the lift. Then I press the button for floor twelve and use the fob again to close the doors and start the lift moving. I use the word "lift" because I heard it in Europe. I don't like the world "lift" like the way I like the word "flat," but I can't imagine ascending to my flat in an elevator.

On the fourth floor the lift stops and a man and a woman get in. The woman is in her early twenties, a little younger than me. The man has to be nearing 50—he's handsome but he has a gut. He presses the button for floor five and touches his security disk to the keypad.

"Do you see *that*," the woman says. "*She's* going to floor *twelve*. Why couldn't *we* get an apartment on floor *twelve*? I bet she has a way better view than we do on floor *five*."

What I don't understand is what they were doing on floor four at 8am if they live on floor five. The pool is on the first floor. The gym is on floor two. The lift stops at floor five and they get off. When I get off at floor twelve, I use the security fob to open my door and breathe a sigh of relief as I enter my flat.

I put the package on the counter and take a CBD cold brew from the refrigerator, along with a sparkling water. I place both on the counter and use my phone to get a photo of them, with the background lighting just right. It was important that I get this apartment because it has both east and north facing windows, and the windows are very large. So in the mornings, I have the sunrise which I can take pictures of and use the light from to post sponsored product photos, and in the evenings I can use the softer but still ample natural light to hop on Instagram live and talk to my followers while I drink a cup of tea. I have this soft off-white robe I wear for these livestreams sometimes. People say it makes them feel like they're in my home, like they're my guests, my friends.

As I alternate drinking the sparkling water and the CBD cold brew, I post the photo, tagging the maker of the coffee. The company that makes the water isn't a sponsor, but I'd like them to be, so I don't tag them. If they see the photo maybe they'll want to be tagged, which they can pay for. After I post the photo I get caught up in scrolling through my feed for a few minutes before I realize what time it. I use a box cutter I keep near the mail holder to open the package. It's just another flat belly tea, and I'm disappointed. I don't do sponsorships with flat belly tea companies anymore. I outgrew that right around the time Arnold told me I was going to be in a movie with George Clooney.

CARLOS

I'm not going to lie: that last fare, Kennedy, was cute as fuck. I liked the way her hair was kind of a mess, and she wasn't wearing any makeup, or at least not that I could tell. I don't know that much about makeup. My mother never wore makeup. Neither did my sisters. My family had other things they needed to spend money on, like food—and clay for my papa's bricklaying business. And the cell phone bill, because without the cell phone bill we couldn't call *Abuela*, who lives in Mexico City with her second husband. My sister, Abril, lives in Mexico City now, too. I guess *she* wears makeup now—she would have to, because last I heard she's some sort of high-class *prostituta*.

And it was obvious that Kennedy was wearing last night's wrinkled clothes. That turns me on, if I'm being honest. If I'm being *really* honest I should tell you that I've only had sex twice. It can be difficult for me to pick up women, so when I meet one who's obviously recently had sex of some kind, it's reassuring for me: to know that women are sexual, that I just need to meet the right one or say the right thing at the right time, that the possibility is there.

But I have a rule: I don't flirt with riders. And anyway, Kennedy is gone now.

I stop at Del Taco and order two Beyond Meat breakfast burritos and a coffee. I'm feeling a little jittery because of the Red Bulls I've already slammed, but my head is killing me. I did I don't know how many grams of cocaine last night, and I drank half a fifth of whisky that Enrique brought to the party.

I have another rule: don't eat in the car. So I'm in the Del Taco sitting at a table with my phone in my hand, scrolling through Facebook. I don't love Facebook, but it's how I keep in touch with my *abuela* and my mom and my cousins. I don't really keep in touch with my sisters.

It's not because I'm Mexican that I'm eating burritos, by the way. Del Taco was just nearby, and it's quick, and I need to get back on the road as soon as possible so I can make some money. I have an audition at 2pm, so I can only drive today until noon. Then I'll need to take a shower and change my clothes and probably rub this caffeine cream I have under my eyes to get rid of the dark circles.

My thumb kind of shakes while I check LinkedIn—which I have only because, I don't know, maybe there's an agent on there I can connect with or something, although that hasn't happened so far, so I mostly just use it to read articles about entrepreneurship from Gary Vaynerchuk and Reid Hoffman— so I decide not to finish the coffee and instead walk up to the counter and order a strawberry lemonade from the cute girl behind the counter. After I place the order, as I'm handing her my debit card, I remember to smile and she smiles back.

"It's a beautiful morning," I say.

"I'm sixteen," she says.

"Okay, that's cool, I guess . . ." I say. But inside I'm saying *fuck* because I can't have that happen again, and why do I have to be such a bad judge of ages? And I think, shouldn't she be in school by now if she's sixteen? But then I remember it's a Sunday.

She hands me the strawberry lemonade.

"Thanks," I say. "Have a . . . nice day." And as quick as I can I make beeline for the door. Only once I'm outside do I remember I left my bag and burrito wrappers on the table and the polite thing would have been to throw them away, but I'm not going back in there.

Another rule I have, which I guess is really just a subset of rule two: don't drink anything but water in the car. But I break it today and get back into the car with my strawberry lemonade.

I affix my phone to the dashboard holder and open the Uber Driver app and tap the button to "Go Online."

Almost immediately, trip requests start coming in. I accept one. The sun is starting to get higher now, so I put on my sunglasses and drive off. I laugh because the address is the same one from which I just picked up my last rider, who was cute as fuck.

ESMERALDA

After breakfast we walk back to the house and Arnold takes off his shirt as soon as we enter. He leaves it in the foyer and I ask him can I get him anything and he says no, he'll be fine.

I follow him into the kitchen, where he picks up his bottle of statins from the counter and shakes it. "Actually, can you get me a glass of water?"

I certainly don't mind getting him a glass of water, so I grab a cup from the cupboard and a pitcher from the fridge and I fill the cup with water from the pitcher. "Do you want some of that CBD oil?" I ask.

"Oh, yeah," he says. "That's probably a good idea."

So I take a bottle of CBD oil from another cupboard and add a few drops—what the bottle says is the right amount of drops for a dose of 25 milliliters—to his water.

"Thank you, Ismi," he says as I hand him the cup. He pops two of the statins into his mouth and drinks half the water. "I'm going to go get some work done."

He takes out his phone and starts dialing a number and brings the phone and the rest of the water outside, to the pool.

It's not terribly warm this morning, but it's not chilly either. Arnold's doctor says he needs to get more sun, and I appreciate that he's trying.

CARLOS

I'm back at the building again, and there's this tall, fit, tan guy with an orange knit cap standing outside it talking at phone. He's holding the phone up in front of his face, with the screen facing him, his arm stretched out. I'm not sure whether this is the guy the Uber Driver app tells me is named Beckett, but when he sees me—or my car, rather, I guess—he nods and looks back at the phone and gives a wave—to the phone, not to me. He opens the rear right-side door and slides into the seat, still talking to the phone.

"—getting into an Uber," he's saying. "I'm gonna go get some coffee and maybe a muffin or something before doing some big things today, so I guess I should sign off now, but—"

I gesture to my phone in the dash holder, trying to confirm the address. You're supposed to confirm the address when the rider gets in—sometimes they type it wrong or think they want to go somewhere but actually want to go somewhere else.

"Yo, hold up," he says to the phone. He lowers his arm and leans over. "Sorry, man—I'm on a livestream. That cool?"

"Sure," I say. I get riders doing livestreams and FaceTimes all the time. It's L.A. It's America. It's the Western world. As long as they're using their phone, it's cool. Only thing I don't like is when someone gets in the car with like a real camera. You gotta pay me if you want to film in my car like that—it's L.A. I've made a few hundred bucks that way. One time two women filmed themselves making out in the back seat while I drove. One time a guy in a dinosaur costume got in with a cameraman. "Just—this right? Marty's Coffee?" I ask.

"Yes, that's right. Thanks, man."

He sits back in the seat and holds the phone out again. "Hey, guys. Y'know what? I was gonna end the stream now, but I feel like talkin' to y'all. We got. Whatta we got?" He looks at the GPS on my phone. "We got eight minutes till we get to this coffee place I'm goin' to, so let's chat a bit. I want to talk to you about the elite. The global elite."

I'm listening.

"So, we all know about this political stuff, right? We got the left and the right and all this shit."

I find myself nodding. The left. The right. That's true.

"But it ain't about that. Not really. What if I told you that the people on the left, like the really big people, the super rich ones, the people with money and fame and all that, are exactly the same as the same people on the right, the rich people? Yo, just last night I was with this chick—you might know her if I said her name, you might not—she's not like, super famous, but she's getting there, maybe. And she's left-wing and shit, right, like I am, right? And she— Nah, nah, we didn't fuck."

It takes me a second, but I realize he's responding to comments that are scrolling by.

"Haha. What do you think? Of course we fucked. That's why I'm not going to tell you who she is. I've got more respect than that. Even if most people in this world don't. Haha. Okay, okay. Back to what I was saying. What was I saying? Right. Yeah. So, like, the elite. They're all in the same league with each other, man, people. Cahoots. That's what I'm trying to tell you. But we can *do* something about that. I don't know about y'all, but *I'm* going to do something about that. Today, in fact. It's gonna be big. It's gonna fuck things up. Me and some . . . some friends . . . are—"

I hear a buzzing sound.

"Yo—hold up, y'all. I'm getting a call. I gotta end the stream. Maybe I'll get back on in a minute. 'Kay, bye. Peace."

This white cargo van in front of me tries to cut me off. I lay on the horn. The guy flips me off but I just drive past him, calmly. "Sorry about that," I say to my passenger. But he has the phone to his ear. I notice that there's a clear difference between the way he talks on the livestream and the way he talks on the phone call.

"Hey. I— What? *What?* You were watching? Oh, come on, I wasn't going to say anything. No, I—"

He's listening to the person on the other end of the line. He listens for a while. I try to turn my attention back to the road.

Finally, he says, soberly, "Okay. Okay. I understand. I'm sorry. I'll be there soon. Okay."

He puts the phone in his lap. With caution, I ask, "Is everything okay?"

"Fine," he says. After a moment, he picks up the phone again. He starts scrolling.

KEELY

I'm coming back to the studio with a cruller and a decaf Americano for J-Sean when I hear screaming coming from inside. It's J-Sean, and the screaming is not like screaming bloody murder, not like he's in trouble or someone is harming him or anything like that. It's yelling. He's yelling words, and I'm used to it by now, but sometimes when he yells his voice can get especially high and shrieky, so I can't help thinking of it as screaming more than yelling. J-Sean is harmless, though, when you get down to it. I've seen him make people cry, and he's hurt feelings pretty bad, but as long as you have thick skin and know what you're getting into, he's harmless.

"Get that out of my fucking face!" he's yelling, and when I walk through the door I see he's waving his hand at Renalda, the intern, who's holding what appears to be a maple cream stick donut from Pappy's Donuts, this place that just opened a couple blocks away and that's getting killer reviews in the papers and local hipster zines and on Yelp. "What are you trying to do, fucking kill me?"

"I don't—" Renalda starts to say.

"Is that gluten free?"

"I—"

"I asked is that fucking gluten free? Is it? Is it gluten free?"

"Well—no. But—"

"Fuck you. Fuck you you fucking . . . you fucking bitch fucking . . . whatever the fuck your name is. Are you trying to kill me? I. Am. Gluten. Fucking. Free."

J-Sean is gluten free and vegan—at least like 70 percent of the time.

"I'm sorry," Renalda says. "I'm—"

I'm standing in the doorway, waiting for the scene to end.

"Just—go," J-Sean says. "Go."

"Am I . . . fired?"

"What? No. Of course not. Are you fucking stupid? Ugh —just get out of here. Find something to do. Go answer my email or something."

"I'm sorry about the—"

"I said GO!"

Renalda makes this little squeak and rushes away from J-Sean on her tiptoes. She sees me and scurries over.

"What happened?" I ask.

"I was just trying to—"

"Oh," I say, "You were just trying to suck up to him."

"I—I see you bring him that every morning. I thought maybe he'd want to try something different." She looks like she's about to cry.

"Hey, you're still learning. You'll get it."

"What should I do with this?" She holds up the stick donut.

"Are they as good as everyone says?"

She shrugs. "Not really."

I shrug. "Eat it, if you want." If she'd said yes, I was maybe going to ask for it.

She makes that squeak again and disappears.

"Here you go," I say to J-Sean, handing him the bag with the cruller in it.

He peaks in the bag, sniffs at it, and then removes the cruller. He takes a bite and then I hand him the Americano. He washes down the bite of cruller and sighs as if he's a smoker who's just taken a long drag after an international flight. "Thank you, Keely. You are a fucking life-saver. The morning I've had."

The cruller, by the way, is not gluten free.

"My pleasure," I say.

He takes another bite, larger. He doesn't wait to swallow before speaking again. "Now—what's up? What's on the schedule? We have that thing with that one girl, yes?"

"Yes. Kennedy Thorne—"

"Kennedy Thorne—right, right—I know her name," he says. He says each syllable of the name right after I do, so we're slightly out of sync but maybe it's possible he does remember her name and wasn't just copying me. "Do you have the dress?"

"It's in the workshop. It's pinned to the mannequin."

"Right, right. Well, go get it please, won't you, darling? I'm going to enjoy my thing and drink my thing. And I'm going to sketch for a few moments so please don't bother me will you? Give me fifteen, yes, darling? Fifteen and then we'll get started."

I wait for him to turn around before I wipe from my blouse the cruller crumbs that were expelled while he talked.

J-Sean's studio is actually this big warehouse space divided into three parts. There's the main studio, where he does things like fittings and meetings and which is wide open, littered with large sketches he's done and paintings he's purchased, and there's a wet bar in one corner. Then there's the workshop, where J-Sean or his assistants, usually his assistants, stitch the fabric, make the clothes, and the workshop is separated from the studio by a large window, so you can see into it, although it's dark in the workshop much of the time so really you can see only vague shapes and shadows. Then, on the second floor, there's J-Sean's loft, where he lives and where his current boyfriend, the artist Stuart Muertez, lives. J-Sean is convinced that Stuart is Banksy, and Stuart lets him believe it, even though, way back in 2003, *The Guardian* described Banksy as white and 28 years old while Stuart is currently, right now, 24 and Hispanic. Poor J-Sean. He has a good heart, a big heart.

I go into the workshop and turn the light on, but the light is dim by default and still it's hard to see things. J-Sean says this is intentional. Says when it comes to fashion "color is secondary to fit, to lines, to curves, to feel." That's a quote from his *Rolling Stone* interview from last winter. The title of the article was "The Influencer: The 32-Year-Old Fashion Mogul You've Probably Never Heard of but Your Kids Just Might Have." There's a copy of the issue framed out in the studio.

I wheel the mannequin with Kennedy Thorne's dress out from the workshop. As I'm push it to the middle of the studio, which is where J-Sean likes to keep the day's active projects, one of his assistants, Maurice, passes me. He smiles and I smile back and he winks. As I push the mannequin past him he slaps me lightly on the ass. Maurice and I hook up sometimes. J-Sean's other assistant, Leilani, has arrived as well. She's at the wet bar filling a glass from the SodaStream. She's dyed her hair blue, I see, since yesterday, and the sides are freshly shaved. "Hey, girl!" she shouts across the studio. She gives me an air-five and I catch it, kiss it, and blow it back to her.

J-Sean is in the opposite corner, sitting in his Herman Miller Eames Lounge, his feet propped on the Ottoman. He's wearing a pair of very large wireless headphones, moving his head a little. His sketchbook is open on his lap but his phone is on top of it and he's scrolling.

I put the mannequin in the center of the studio and realize I don't know where Renalda went. It's almost nine and and the space is coming to life.

J-Sean shrieks. "The fuck!" He jumps from the chair, nearly spilling the decaf Americano he's set on the floor, and rips the headphones from his head. "Keely." he says. "Keely!"

I wave at him and he spots me.

He storms over, waving his phone. "Tell me it isn't true," he says. "Tell me that my very own eyes do deceive me."

"What's that, J-Sean?"

He shoves his phone into my hands. "I was just sitting in my chair over there. Eating my thing. Drinking my thing. Minding *my own business*. When I decide to check out this Kennedy Thorne girl who's coming over. First off, did you know she has 400,000 Instagram followers?"

"Yeah," I say.

"Well that's cool and all, although it's a little low for my taste." J-Sean doesn't usually design for anyone with less than a million, but if I remember right, Kennedy Thorne's agent was able to get him a bottle of a very expensive and rare tequila that he had his eye on.

"Right," I say.

"But—and I am going to *scream* about this—I am going to *fall apart*—she doesn't follow me."

I look down at his phone. "I'm sure that's just a mistake —"

"SHE DOESN'T FOLLOW ME! SHE DOESN'T FOLLOW ME! SHE DOESN'T FUCKING FOLLOW ME!"

BECKETT

I consider asking the Uber drive to skip the coffee shop and just take me to what we've come to refer to as headquarters, but I'm really high-strung right now. I don't know whether it's the coke that I did last night before we fucked, or the coke I did after we fucked, or whether it's what's going on later today, but I'm just really jittery and I can feel my heart beating. I feel it in my arms, though, not my chest. I can feel my heart driving the blood through my veins, pushing it up my chest and into my shoulders and down my brachia. Again I want to open one of them, one of the veins, and just release the pressure before it's expelled through my fingertips.

I'm really high-strung but the coffee shop we're going to has this CBD coffee that's supposed to chill you out. I left my vape at home. I should have brought it, should have let my old friend indica do her thing and take care of me. I thought of it before leaving the apartment, but I didn't want my mind in any sort of altered state today. But let's face it: an altered state is what I'm in. Altered states are unavoidable.

I'd set the livestream's recording to stay up for 24 hours, so I go into the app and delete it manually. Anders is right. I shouldn't have gone online today, not live like that. Today is a day for laying low—until we don't. But until we don't, we have to.

We get to Marty's Coffee and I ask the driver to wait outside. "Can you do that, like a cab? Can you wait for me so I don't have to call another Uber?"

"Sure thing. I have to charge you, though. The thing will keep running. I couldn't not charge you even if I wanted to."

That's fine. Money is no object when you're already 100 grand in credit card debt. Not to mention student loans you never plan on paying off. I burned through the last of my trust fund back in May. I go into the coffee shop.

The line is longer than I expected. But I guess it's Sunday. I have this way of losing track of what day it is. Especially on the weekends, when Friday blurs into Saturday blurs into Sunday, depending on who I'm with and what drugs I'm doing. This is California and most people don't go to church on Sundays in California. They go to coffee shops and Russian spas and hiking in the canyon and probably to brothels and raves. So there are more people here than I was thinking. I think about leaving. But I'm here, and there's the barista. She's got nice tits. They're popping out of her light blue blouse and her green apron. She has big round glasses I'd like to cum on. I get in line.

In front of me is this woman with two young children, a boy and girl. I bet you a million bucks she's the nanny, not the mom. Parents are probably off in Spain or Italy or something drinking wine and making love. Or the parents are like Jennifer Aniston and whoever Jennifer Aniston's husband is, and they can't be bothered with the kids today because they have to get ready for their precious award ceremony. I feel bad for the children. I feel deeply bad for them. Their situation breaks my heart.

"Can I get a bagel?" the girl says. "With strawberry cream cheese?"

The boy tugs on the leg of the nanny's pants. "I want one, too."

"Perfect," the nanny says. "You can share one. You can each have half."

"But I want a whole one!" the girl says.

"Me too!"

"Could you *eat* a whole one?" The nanny looks at the boy. "Could *you*?"

After a second, they both shake their heads.

"See—so you'll share one. Doesn't that make sense?"

"Okay."

"Okay."

Poor kids. Their parents are multimillionaires and the kids aren't even allowed a whole bagel to themselves.

In front of the trio is a Hasidic Jew. I don't even want to look at him.

Past the Hasidic Jew is a black guy in a tank top. Fit. Lean. Looks like a runner. He's wearing running shorts and a stainless steel smart watch and white running shoes. Probably just finished a run. Or in the middle of a run, stopping for a coffee. He's looking at the menu. Squinting. My guess is he wears glasses but didn't take them on his run. Forgot to put his contacts in because his vision isn't *that* bad.

The young woman in front of him is a little chubby. Not too chubby but not model material. I can't see her face from back here but probably I'd like to cum on it, too.

I'm good at reading people. One look at someone and I can tell you their story.

Poor kids and their fucking celebrity parents who don't fucking care.

I take out my phone. I feel like my eyes are enormous and everyone can see them.

I don't tweet much but I have a couple hundred thousand followers. I have almost a million on Instagram. I'm not going to tweet now but I do open Twitter and search for my name. There are people talking about how I went on some sort of racist rant a few minutes ago and then deleted it. Some sort of meltdown, this guy with a blue check mark says. An alt-right tirade, says another. I was live for maybe 15 minutes. A reporter from BuzzFeed is calling me a Nazi. One guy is standing up for me and saying I'm just woke. He's using the word ironically, is my impression. Some bitch with a blue checkmark is calling me the next PewDiePie. Someone suggests I go on Joe Rogan's podcast. Someone else calls for @jack to ban me, ban me now.

In my hand my phone shatters and blood pours between my finger tips. But not really. That's just want I want to happen, but I'm not strong enough to break my phone, not with one hand.

I don't know how long I've been in line but the Hasidic Jew is ordering now. Aren't they not supposed to be out on Sundays? There's CBD cold brew and *nitro* CBD cold brew and

I don't know which one I want. It's 9am. I hear a commotion behind me.

KENNEDY

When I enter J-Sean Laurentius's studio in the Wholesale District it's clear something is wrong. The big dreary studio space is mostly empty and dead silent, but I can hear muffled yelling and and maybe even crying from above. I look around for someone to speak to. I see no one. Then out of nowhere this girl appears. She's like nineteen. "Hi," she says. "You must be Ms. Thorne."

"You can call me Kennedy."

"I'm Renalda. J-Sean is . . . indisposed . . . but I'm sure he'll be down shortly. Very shortly. Um—can I get you a drink or take your jacket?"

The girl's eyes are red, puffy. I hand her my denim jacket. "I don't think I've met you," I say. "I don't think you were here when I did my original fitting."

"I'm new. I've been an intern for J-Sean for just a few weeks. Can I get you a drink?"

"I'm okay," I say.

It's clear the girl doesn't know what to do next. Neither do I, but I get the feeling I'm supposed to be the grown-up here, so I ask her if I can vape while I wait. Outside.

"Sure. Of course," she says.

"Would you like to come with me?"

"That would be great."

She tells me they don't vape out front because the sidewalk is so small and then there's the road right there and you technically can't vape or smoke or anything like that less than 50 feet away from a building, so she takes me through a side door and into an alley where no one can see from the road.

"Fewer," I tell her as I take out my JUUL.

"I'm sorry?" she says.

I take a drag and savor the mango flavor. "It's 50 feet or *fewer* away from the side the building, not less." I hand her the vape pen.

"Oh. Right." She takes a drag. Then another. Then she hands it back to me.

We stand there for a while. A minute or two. Or thirty seconds. I think I see a rat scurry behind a dumpster, but I'm not positive it was a rat. There's one half of a pair of Converse All-Stars—or maybe it's a knock-off—a few feet away.

"Actually," Renalda says, "actually, I'm sorry, but that's wrong. It doesn't matter whether you say less or fewer. For a long time, everybody, *everybody*, said less, whether they were talking about countable items or not. And then in 1770 this guy named Baker was all like, I think it should be this other way instead, and for some reason everyone listened to him, even though he said 'I think' and had no real authority to make a decision like that."

"Oh?" I said.

"Yeah. So. I mean, use fewer if you want. That's fine. But don't do it because you think you have to."

"Huh," I said, taking another drag.

"I used to be an English major."

"Ah."

"But I dropped out after this talent agent found me and said I should be a model."

"Oh?" She probably *could* be a model.

She shrugs. "Yeah. Turned out he was a sleaze, though. But then I got an internship with J-Sean."

"I dropped out too," I tell her for some reason.

She looks at her Apple Watch. "J-Sean is coming back downstairs. We should go in."

"Okay," I say, putting away my JUUL.

"Thanks for sharing, by the way," she says.

"No problem," I say.

"It's just that I'm trying to quit smoking, like completely quit smoking, and I haven't had any nicotine in forever, and that was just so good."

"No problem," I say again.

KEELY

J-Sean is upstairs masturbating. Calming him down was a struggle. Calming J-Sean down is always a struggle. But it's also always doable. I've gotten good at it. It's a big part of my job description. First I took him upstairs to the loft, where Stuart was still asleep. I told him that, with regards to the Kennedy Thorne not following him thing, it was probably just a misunderstanding. She probably accidentally unfollowed him. Or Mark Zuckerberg hacked her account and made her unfollow him. Remember how you think they shadowbanned you after you posted that photo of that shirt with Donald Trump's face on it that you made? I asked him. Then I reminded him that Kennedy Thorne is not a new client. He's been working with her for weeks. This is her second fitting. He's met with her before and it didn't matter then whether she followed him or not. Then, just as he was quieting down, I slapped him across the face, hard, and told him to jack off as quickly as possible and then come back downstairs. Stuart didn't stir—who knows what time he went to bed and what drugs he took last night. Barbiturates, at least, and probably Xanax. Who knows whether he'll wake up.

Now I'm at the wet bar handing Kennedy Thorne a raspberry CBD sparkling water and asking her if she can please do me a personal favor and follow J-Sean on Instagram and Twitter. At least Instagram, please.

"I'm afraid I don't use Twitter," she says, taking out her phone.

"That's okay. I can explain that to him. Just Instagram, then—please."

"Sure thing." She taps her screen a few times. She has one of the big phones and it's infuriating in her small, veiny hands. "Let me just—what—?"

She trails off. She squints. I think she's going to drop the beverage. "Is everything okay?"

"Fine," she says. "Just . . . fine . . ." She makes a few more taps. "There," she says cheerfully. She clicks the phone to sleep and drops it into her blood-red handbag.

"Thank you!" I tell her, and I am grateful. I never *enjoy* slapping J-Sean. "Renalda—can you take Kennedy over to the dress. I'm sure J-Sean will be down in—"

I hear his large feet thudding behind me down the staircase, which is next to the wet bar. I turn around just as he says, "Ladies! Forgive my indisposition. I forgot about an urgent matter and now I've taken care of it and we have a dress to finish off! Ms. Thorne! It's a pleasure to see you again." He takes her hand and kisses it. Then he kisses her cheek. As Renalda leads her over to the dress J-Sean looks at me.

"Totally shadowbanned," I tell him under my breath. "She *was* following you and it just randomly unfollowed."

"I knew it. Fucking Jack."

"Zuck. Jack is Twitter."

"Fucking Zuck, then. Zucking fucker. They're all the same person anyway."

"Did you wash your hands?" I ask.

"Of *course.*"

I don't believe him. We follow Renalda and Kennedy Thorne over to the dress.

KENNEDY

I am not certain I saw what I thought I saw when I opened Instagram to follow J-Sean Laurentius.

What I thought I saw was multiple posts that were photos of Beckett with captions like *I can't believe it* and *Say it isn't so*.

I am standing in the center of the studio. There are people surrounding me. I have my arms out. My sweater and pants have been removed. And then my shirt. "Do you mind," J-Sean asks, "if we also remove the bra? It can stay on if you want but you're going to need to take it off eventually when you put the dress on for the red carpet, so we're going to get the most accurate measurements now, if you take it off now. Plus, I promise you—all the men here are like hella gay, so it's like, no biggie."

"No problem," I tell him. I reach back behind myself and undo the clasp. One of J-Sean's female assistants slides the left strap from my shoulder, then the right strap. I pull my arms through and now I'm standing nearly naked in the middle of J-Sean Laurentius's studio. The studio is both lit and dark at the same time. Colors are accurate and details are clear, but shadows are emphasized. I think about how I probably look pretty good right now. I could take a mirror selfie, cover my tits with one arm.

"Arms back out please."

I extend my arms again.

"Here," J-Sean says, pointing to my waist.

A young man with bleached blond hair and tattoos covering his forearms wraps a yellow measuring tape around my midsection at the belly button.

"Here," J-Sean says again.

The measuring tape is wrapped around my ass.

"Here."

Just above my ass, between my ass and my waist.

"Here."

My rib cage.

"Here."

My breasts, at the nipples. My nipples go hard at the touch of the measuring tape. I breathe, try to force them to soften.

"Arms down, please."

I lower my arms.

"Here."

The measuring tape is around my shoulders.

"Wait. Never mind. The dress doesn't have shoulders. Silly me. Silly J-Sean."

The assistants laugh.

"Cool. Cool. Thanks, Kennedy. Beautiful. You're beautiful. You can relax for a minute. Ima take a look at these measurements."

"Would you like a robe?" Keely asks.

I tell her no, that's okay, as I relax the muscles of my body.

Renalda hands me my drink—the sparkling raspberry CBD water and gin. When nobody was looking, I added gin from their wet bar. "Can I get you anything?"

"Another one of these," I say, and I down what's left in the glass in one swallow, sad that the next one won't have gin.

My phone is in my handbag on a chair a few feet away, which I see is also where my clothes ended up, and I do not reach for it to verify what I think I've seen.

Renalda returns with another drink and I thank her and take a sip. J-Sean returns and I hand the drink back to Renalda.

"So, girl," J-Sean says, "you on the keto diet or what? Because these numbers are all just a little smaller than last time, except your ass, which is a tad bigger and just beautiful."

"Peloton," I tell him.

"Nice. I don't have one of those, but lots of people talk about them."

"I have one," Keely says. "I like it."

"Nice. Anyway—let's get this dress on you, yeah?"

I am being manipulated like a doll. I lift my legs as commanded, first one, then the other. I raise and lower my arms. A zipper somewhere is zipped, a hook clasped. The dress is on.

"Oh it's just gorgeous," J-Sean says. "Go-or-geous. Isn't it beautiful?"

"It's beautiful," Renalda says.

J-Sean doesn't look at her. "Not you. Keely, isn't it beautiful?"

"It's beautiful," Keely says. "You're an artist, J-Sean."

"I *am* an artist. You, Not-Keely, go get a mirror."

Renalda wheels over a full-length mirror and I see myself in the dress.

"What do you *think*?" J-Sean says, and I realize I haven't said anything.

"It's *perfect*," I tell him. "It's great!"

"Now, it's not quite perfect, not yet. I need to take this in an inch here, and also here, and I want to make just a slight alteration here to show off a bit more of those glutes you've been working on, but—lift up your arms for me again—right, hmmm, okay, so I need to just make a slight adjustment here"—he sticks a pin into the dress somewhere under my armpit—"but otherwise . . . yeah, perfect. Keely, dear?"

Keely is helping me out of the dress. "So you'll come back at 2:30 and we'll have these alterations all made and get you suited up one last time just in time for the Red Carpet. Sound good?"

"Sounds good," I say.

"Oh, I am just so *excited*," J-Sean says. "I've never been on *the* Red Carpet, but I love when my stuff shows up on a red carpet. *Any* red carpet. I just love them *all*."

When I'm dressed and my bag is slung over my arm, Keely says, "We called an Uber for you, on us—just tell them where you want to go."

"Wait wait wait wait wait," says J-Sean. "Real quick. Let's get a *selfie*. Two selfies, yeah? I tag you, you tag me?"

He has his arm around me and he's making a sign with his hands and snapping a photo with his phone. Then he hands the camera to Keely and she takes a photo of us too. I get out my phone and see there are several notifications, including two missed calls and a text from Arnold. I press the camera button and hand the phone to Keely, who snaps a couple photos.

"Beautiful," J-Sean says. "Gorgeous. I'll see you later. Kiss kiss." He kisses my cheek. "Delightful," he says.

Renalda walks me to the exit and as I'm leaving I hear J-Sean yelling "Keely! Keely! Where is my GRAPEFRUIT? I'm getting peckish!"

Renalda tells me the Uber is a red Tesla Model 3 and sure enough there's one waiting at the curb. I thank her and she gives me this sort of sad look. I get in the car and I give the driver Arnold's address, which I have to look up on my phone, and then I look at Arnold's text.

Did you make it to J-Sean Laurentius's? it says.

Yes, I type back. Then, *I'm coming over.*

Why? I receive almost instantly.

I don't know, but I am, I send. Then, *Did you hear about Beckett?*

He doesn't respond right away. Seeing as I don't actually know about Beckett, I open Instagram. At first I am not confronted with his photo. In fact, I'm confronted with a photo of myself, with J-Sean Laurentius, and I look very happy. I scroll down, past a picture of a dog, another picture of a dog, a picture of a sunset or a sunrise, a picture of Daniel Craig . . . and it seems like for a moment I'm not going to see what I thought I saw—but then I do. Beckett's face, in black and white, a photo of him I've seen before, and the caption says, *I have no words Rest In Peace you beautiful soul.*

I realize I'm going about this the wrong way and I open my phone's browser and Google "Beckett Shaw."

One headlines says: FAMED YOUTUBER BECKETT SHAW DEAD

Another says: YOUTUBER BECKETT SHAW KILLED IN BROAD DAYLIGHT

Another: POPULAR YOUTUBER BECKETT SHAW, ONE OTHER, SHOT BY MASKED GUNMEN

And there's another one that says BECKETT SHAW, FAMOUS YOUTUBER, IN CRITICAL CONDITION, which gives me hope but when I click on it and read the article I see that Beckett died at the scene.

I swipe backward at my phone. Another headline: TWO DEAD, ONE INJURED, IN L.A. COFFEE SHOP SHOOTING

I tap the headline and Beckett is one of the two dead. There's a photo of the outside of Marty's Coffee, a couple cop cars, an ambulance, a stretcher.

I get a new text from Arnold that says *Oh my god!*

I don't reply right away.

Have you had breakfast? Arnold asks. *We could get an early lunch.*

I wasn't planning on eating today, not until one of the afterparties. *We could do that.*

Ismi is taking a nap. Let's meet at the cafe around the corner from my house. How far away are you?

I ask the driver. *Fifteen minutes, depending on traffic*, I tell Arnold.

Perfect. I need to put my shirt on. I'll see you soon.

I ask the driver whether there's a cafe near our destination.

"The fuck?" he says. "I don't know. You got an address?"

"Never mind," I tell him. "Just, when we get there, drive around the block until we find it."

I need some CBD or some reishi or ashwaganda or something. Hell, I'd even take some ketamine right about now, and I *swear* I'm not a drug person.

EV & GWEN

This is DINO. DINO is a peer-to-peer distributed social network built upon a node.js framework. To use DINO, send a message to @Ev using Scuttlebutt. @Ev will forward your request over a secure, encrypted connection to @Gwen, who will send you an invite via email (please provide your email address when messaging @Ev via Scuttlebutt) with a link to set up your own DINO distro. @Ev will respond to your initial Scuttlebutt message with your own personal DINO decryption key. Please keep this key handy. You will need it whenever you log on to DINO. In the event you lose your DINO decryption key, we will not be able to generate a new one. Your DINO @ name will be lost and you will have to restart the process.

Note: to do the above, you will need a device with command line access. No iPhones here.

@Ev Post-yoga conversation with @Gwen this morning. We were drinking smoothies. Gwen's recipe. Talking about cyborgs. Distribution. Confluence. Whether the big blech companies (TW, FB, GOOG, APPL) even know what they're doing anymore. Have they lost self-awareness? Did they ever have self-awareness?

@Gwen @Ev I was telling you I don't think rogue conglomerates are capable of self-awareness. Never were and never will be.

@Ev @Gwen And then I said, "conglomerates"? Didn't those go the way of the mainframe decades ago?

@Gwen @Ev Right. You did say that. Then you got an erection and we got caught up in something and lost the thread of the conversation.

@Ev

@Gwen Teehee

@Gwen Talking with Ev this morning and I inadvertently used the world "conglomerate" when referring to the big blech companies and at first I thought it was a mistake but then after meditating for a bit I realized it wasn't inadvertent at all. Just my soul's expulsion of something we've all known deep inside for half a decade now. Alphabet. Moonshots. Search engines. What's an engine anyway. Video platforms. Bluetube (because it gives me the blues). Image search. Safe search off. Pornography.

@Ev Apple. Banana. iPad. iPhone. Pro. Mini. Crackbook. Music. DieTunes. CrapStore. Give me a break. Gwen is right (see this thread: /#df3335). Too many fingers in the cheesecake. Tentacles in the custard. It's like Hentai porn.

@**Gwen** Thinking about what Ev said in that post up there (/#df5665). FB is like Hentai porn. In Japan "Hentai" means perversion. Any perversion. "Porn" is redundant. Ev might be right.

@**Ev** @Gwen Is Hentai supposed to be capitalized? I think I had that wrong.

@**Gwen** @Ev If I remember right from my time in Japan before the bookstore burned down it is supposed to be capitalized.

@**Ev** @Gwen I looked it up. See link. /**177932 Not capitalized.

@**Gwen** Thinking about capitalization. Remembering the idea raised by others that as a form of hierarchical expression capitalization is oppressive. Elitist. Demonstrative of a desire to claim superiority over another. Remembering now that bell hooks said she chose her pen name to emphasize her writing over who she is. Curious, though: musn't we work harder than ever to keep a grasp on our identity?

@**Gwen** Made delicious smoothies post-yoga, but pre-sex, this morning. Recipe was: 1/2 cup coconut milk, 1/2 banana, 1 egg, 1/2 avocado, large handful spinach, 1/2 tbsp pure cacao powder, Cordyceps extract, lion's mane extract, honey to taste, ice. @Ev said tasted like a "liquid hard-on."

@Ev Link: /**88322 Death of another Influencer this morning, allegedly. This one not a suicide. Appears to have been a very public murder. A physical manifestation of TW-mob violence, perhaps?

@Gwen @Ev Just finished reading about that. I mean, details seem sparse right now. Seems to me like a wrong-place-wrong-time sort of incident. A child was also killed. A robbery gone wrong, perhaps. Or a vendetta against the owner of that coffee shop. A former employee, maybe?

@Ev @Gwen Article says there were two shooters. Two former employees?

@Gwen @Ev It all happened like 16 minutes ago. Reports unsubstantiated. My guess probably just one shooter.

@Ev @Gwen I'm calling it: Guy should have gotten off the Internet. Read a book. Done some yoga. Moved to North Dakota. His is not the last Influencer death we'll see.

@Gwen @Ev Today?

@Ev

@Gwen Today. Tomorrow. Until the world dies with all of us on it.

@**Gwen** @Ev You're so nihilistic.

@**Ev** @Gwen We're all totally fucked.

@**Ev** Getting ready for my shift at the Casselton Ruby Tuesday. Still wishing they'd pay me in crypto.

@**Gwen** @Ev Love you.

MARTY

The cop has taken over my office at the back of the coffee shop but also he won't let me leave. Says he needs a "base of operations, ma'am" and I'm just going to have to give the LAPD what they need for the next few hours if I don't mind thank you very much. I do mind, not because I don't want to help—I want to help—but because there is blood on my face and my glasses and my blue blouse and he won't let me wash it off. Says it's evidence. Says the medical examiner will take a look at me shortly, see whether I'm okay and whether any of blood is my own or just the victims' and what it can tell them about the case. I tell him none of the blood is my own. Tell him I would know if I'd been shot. Tell him I wasn't shot but that please I would like to just go outside into some fresh air or something because I just witnessed—

Hold that thought, he says. Says we need to save that for the official interview.

I ask him can't he just do the official interview right now?

Not yet, he says. Say he has to follow a specific procedure. Says he's waiting for his partner to show up and then they can both sit down and talk to me for a few minutes.

I ask him am I in trouble or something?

'Course not, he says. Witness reports say nothing about you doing the shooting.

I ask him wait a minute—you've already talked to other witnesses?

Done a few little interviews, he says.

But if you've done a few other interviews why can't you just interview me now so I can go take a shower and crawl into bed for the next week and cry?

He says it's just procedure. Says the witnesses were out there in the cafe and I'm back here in the office and they—the detectives—are making their way back here one step at a time.

The fuck? I say. I'm back here 'cause you put me back here.

I don't make the rules, he says. He's taking notes on his iPad with a stylus. Turning my office into his "base of operations" seems to entail just bringing his iPad back here and his cup of coffee, which he did not get from my shop but from Starbucks. There's a Starbucks cup in my office.

Then he says, And please don't swear, ma'am.

I remind him that my preferred pronouns are he and his—that is to say, sir—and he says Oh, right, and apologizes and tells me about his nephew who's transitioning. This is the second time I've heard about the nephew, so I know the detective will probably call me ma'am again soon but I won't blame him or take it personally.

I look down and there's something beige on my dark gray pants, mixed with tacky, drying blood. Instinct tells me to flick it off and so I move to, putting my thumb and middle finger together, but then instead I pinch it and it's fleshy and squishy and I realize it's a chunk of skin from somewhere. Some part of maybe an ear or a face, and it's a very light beige, which tells me it doesn't belong to the guy I saw get shot, who the detective told me was a famous YouTuber. It belongs probably to—

I'm freaking out now. You okay? the detective asks, looking up from his iPad.

I'm gonna throw up, I tell him.

He looks around. He grabs my garbage can. Here, he says, holding it out to me. Use this.

The garbage can is made of black mesh wire and if I vomit into it the vomit will not be contained. I stand. Let me out, I say.

I'm sorry but procedure—

Let me the fuck out! I grab the door handle and of course I'm not actually being legally detained so it opens and I practically stumble out into the cafe and I'm not surprised by the scene but still.

I dive behind the counter and vomit into one of the big trash cans. I vomit and vomit some more. Eventually I'm dry heaving over the garbage can and I stand and focus on my breath and my throat is sore and my chest hurts.

The detective or cop or whatever he is is talking to a woman who's wearing rubber gloves. Did she just contaminate the crime scene? he asks her.

Oh, shut up, Paul, she says. Somebody get this girl a glass of water.

Boy, I think, but don't say. Then I correct myself—man.

Someone shoves a glass of water into my hand and I drink it wholly. Finally I stand tall.

In my coffee shop are the woman with the rubber gloves, the detective, several other cops, another woman with rubber gloves and a man with rubber gloves. On the floor is the YouTuber Beckett Shaw, whose videos I've never seen but know of only because the detective asked me What do you know about the YouTuber Beckett Shaw? His eyes are closed. There's blood pooled around him in a big sticky mess. The blood is dark and deep and I cannot see the floor tile through it. There's so much of it. I can tell it stopped flowing a while ago but I can also tell that when it was flowing it was flowing from the YouTuber Beckett Shaw's neck, which the man with the rubber gloves is bent down near, with a camera, taking pictures of. Next to the YouTuber Beckett Shaw is a little girl with blonde hair—or I guess the body of a little girl with blonde hair—whose eyes are open and whose blonde hair is partly in Beckett Shaw's blood and who is missing part of one cheek and who looks so very very small.

I feel vomit welling up again. I lean over the trash can.

I feel a hand on my back and the detective says: I just didn't want you to have to see all this, kid.

MARTY

Some time passes. I don't know how long. I guess it's just a few minutes. My head is swimming for most of it. I'm staring at my own vomit in the garbage can and I'm sitting on the floor behind the bar. I can hear noises on the other side, sounds. They're indistinct. Then they become more clear: voices, emanating from people who are doing their jobs. They're sober voices, but also unaffected. I stand.

The detective is on the other side of the cafe talking to a new, female detective. "Hey—you okay, kid?" he says when he sees me. "You were kind of just . . . down there."

I nod.

"She's not a kid, Paul," says the woman. She looks at me. "Can anyone get you anything?"

I shake my head. "I'm going to make myself an espresso."

"I don't know if—" Paul starts to say.

"Let her make a damn espresso, Paul," says the woman. "It's not going to contaminate anything." She looks at me again. "But then we're going to have to ask you a few questions, okay. And then after that we can get you out of here."

"Thank you," I say.

I turn to the silver espresso machine. Then I change my mind and turn to the burr grinder. I grind some Guatemalan beans. They're my favorite right now. When someone comes in and says what's your favorite right now, I say "The Guatemalan." A Jewish customer was paying for his Guatemalan Americano when. . . .

I put the coffee grounds in the portafilter. I take the hand tamp and tamp the grounds into the basket. I keep my arm at a 90-degree angle and make sure to use 30 pounds of pressure. I use a white cloth to wipe the excess grounds from around the edge of the basket. I purge the espresso machine. I insert the portafilter into the group head. I pull the lever, slowly, pulling the water through the grounds. I count the seconds. The extraction lasts for 22 seconds. The crema on top of the coffee is a deep rust color. A perfect pull. I put the shot mug with the espresso shot in it on a dish. Then I grab an 8-ounce glass and fill it with seltzer water. "I'm done," I say. "Would anyone like anything?"

Paul looks around. The medical investigators look at him and the woman detective. The woman detective says, "No, thank you. I think everyone's okay."

I down the espresso shot in one gulp. I pick up the seltzer water. "Let's go back to my office, then."

My office is not meant to accommodate three people. I take my chair. Paul starts to take the other chair and then hesitates and lets the woman take it. I sip my seltzer water. Then I put the glass down next to Paul's iPad. Paul picks up the iPad.

"I understand it's been a rough day," the woman says. "We're going to make this quick."

I nod.

"You're the owner?"

I nod. "Marty," I say. "Preferred pronouns are— It doesn't matter."

"Sure it does. Go ahead."

"He, him, his," I say.

"I told him about my nephew who's transitioning," Paul says.

The woman ignores him. "I'm Detective Ramos. You can call me Adeline. How old are you, Marty?"

"Twenty-seven."

"How long have you owned this place?"

"Um—seventeen months. I opened it 17 months ago."

"It has solid Yelp reviews," Paul says.

Adeline glowers at him.

"*What?* Four and a half stars."

Adeline looks back at me. "You were behind the counter during the shooting?"

I nod. "I was making an Americano for this Jewish man. Three shots."

"Of espresso," Adeline says.

I nod. "Yeah."

Paul is making notes on his iPad.

"Also three gunshots," I say.

Paul looks up. "One of the other witnesses said there were only two."

"Right," Adeline says. "And both hit their targets."

"Presumed targets," Paul says.

"I don't think the girl was a target," I say. "I mean, why would someone just shoot a little girl?" I choke as I say this, because I remember that some of the girl's flesh was on my apron.

"Why would they shoot a fairly uncontroversial YouTuber?" Paul asks.

"He wasn't exactly uncontroversial," Adeline says. "He was a known conspiracy theorist. He was involved in Gamergate, before he got popular. And he retweeted something about Pizzagate, even, I'm told."

Paul shrugs. "I watch his stuff. I thought the guy was just funny."

"Anyway," Adeline says to me, "you're *sure* there were three shots?"

I nod. "Yes. The two guys came into the cafe, side by side. I remember because I was giving the Jewish customer a lid, and as I looked up I see these two guys come in side by side, and they're struggling to fit through the door together. I remember thinking, why didn't they walk in single file? I know that was stupid of me to think, because it was the *first* thing I thought when I saw them. I didn't think, at least not at first, Hey, it's strange that those guys are wearing masks, which, like, who the hell doesn't notice that sort of thing *right away*?"

"So they were wearing the masks when they entered the shop?"

"Yes. I'm sure of it."

"We have one witness who says they put the masks on once they got inside," Paul says. "Says they were two blond guys."

I shake my head. "No. They definitely had the masks on before. I watched them come in."

"Another witness says one of the guys was a woman, says it was a butch lesbian with big tits and a—"

"*Paul,*" Adeline says.

"*What?* I'm just saying what one of the witnesses—"

"Paul, shut up. Marty, you are sure they were wearing masks from the time they entered?"

"Yes," I say again.

"Would be nice if you had some security cameras in this joint," Paul says.

"Shut the fuck up, Paul. For God's sake."

I'm starting to feel attracted to Detective Ramos, even though I hate cops.

"I haven't been able to justify the cost of one, I guess," I say. Although now I wonder whether a security camera would have been a better use of credit than paying influencers to post on social media. "Anyway, they were wearing the masks, so it wouldn't help."

"Paul," Adeline says, "is going to sit quietly and take notes now. Marty, please continue. Can you tell me how the rest of the scene played out?"

I nod. I wonder how much detectives count as cops, when it comes to their complicity with fascism. I also wonder whether Adeline is single—or maybe polyamorous, at least. She isn't wearing a ring. "The two guys come in, wearing masks"—

Paul starts to say something; Adeline gives him an icy look; Paul looks back at his iPad; I decide I'm going to ask Detective Ramos out when this interview is over—"and then I notice, immediately after noticing the masks, that they are both holding guns. One of the guys, the one on my right, so I guess if you were them then the one on the left, raises his gun and fires at the little girl. People started screaming and getting up from their tables. The other guy said—and I remember this clearly because I thought it was strange—'Dude, what the fuck?' and then he raises his own gun and fires, and I hear the bullet ping off of something, maybe something metal, probably something metal. Then he says 'Fuck' and goes to shoot again, but the other guy pushes down on his arm and raises his own gun, then he shoots and the . . . the YouTuber guy goes down. He landed on the nanny of the little girl, who was on the ground too, screaming at the little girl."

"She was covered in blood, the nanny," Adeline says. "She sprained her wrist."

"Yeah, he kind of landed on her, and then rolled off." My eyes are watering because I'm thinking about all the blood and the guy and the little girl lying there together.

"Can we get you anything?" Detective Ramos asks. She puts a hand on my hand, which is on my leg. "Water?"

I shake my head. I gesture to the seltzer water on my desk. "I'm okay. Um . . . then I ducked down behind the counter as fast as I could. I mean, I guess I should have ducked down earlier, right? Like when I first saw the gun. Or when the first shot went off. But . . . but I was just stunned, I guess, for a second."

"So you didn't see the gunmen leave?"

I shake my head. I'm suddenly having trouble speaking, breathing. There are tears running down my face. Detective Ramos takes my head and presses it into her breasts and strokes my hair. She says something to Paul about needing to find the second bullet that was fired, the one that missed. Paul says the *alleged* second bullet. Adeline says she's going to pull Paul off the case and have him put on probation if he doesn't shut the fuck up and go look for it.

She tells me everything is going to be okay. I tell her all I want to do is take a shower.

CARLOS

One of the men is sitting in my front seat with a semi-automatic pistol in his lap—his hand resting on it but not quite primed to pull the trigger—pointing in my general direction. He's not quite primed to pull the trigger but my general sense is that he could be primed within a fraction of a second, if I were to attempt any funny business. He reminds me not to attempt any funny business, and his partner in the back seat, who's staring at his phone, says, "Can you please for fuck sake stop calling it 'funny business'? You're not a fuckin' . . . a fuckin' . . . God damn I don't know what but you're not some sort of fuckin' cheesy fuck. And he knows, dammit. He *knows*. You've told him like seven times and you have a gun pointed at him. Guy's not an idiot."

The man in the passenger seat prods my leg with the gun. "You an idiot?"

"I— I—" I say.

"See. I think he is an idiot."

"He's not a fuckin' idiot, Juan. And you best remember he's driving this car and if you shoot him it'll be just as bad as if he tried anything. He'd lose control and either we'd die or if we didn't die we'd still crash and people'd see us." Then he taps me hard on the back of my neck. "Don't get any ideas, though. I'm not saying you should try something just so we'd get caught. Probably if you tried something we'd all die, you included."

Probably we'd all die because we're cruising down the 5 doing exactly the speed limit. There's just enough traffic that there's hardly a few car lengths between cars, but not so much traffic that you can't do exactly the speed limit. We're doing exactly the speed limit because the man in the back seat told me to drive as fast as I could without exceeding the speed limit.

The man in the back seat also has a gun. I am under no illusions that he doesn't, that he's kind, that he wouldn't pop me in a second if he felt the situation called for it.

Or if he felt I was no longer useful.

Both men are wearing masks.

"You know who's the fuckin' idiot, Juan?" the man in the back seat says. "You fuckin' are. You didn't fuckin' shoot anybody back there. You shot like, what, an ice machine?"

"Me? *I* didn't shoot anything? You shot a little girl, man! What the fuck was that?! Girl was like six years old, four years old! You just popped her in the face."

"Listen—I did what I had to do. We couldn't go in there and *just* kill Shaw, okay."

"Why *not?* Anders said the target was Shaw. He didn't say nothing about killing anybody else, certainly not any kids. We were supposed to rob the place."

"The line was longer than I expected, okay? We got in there, and Shaw was too far back in line. If we'd robbed the place, like went up to the counter, Shaw might have run while we were up there, and I couldn't shoot him first and *then* rob the place—we'd be in there too long after hitting the target. That could cause all sorts of complications. So I improvised."

"You improvised by shooting a little kid in the face!"

"Listen—now we just look like sadistic randos, right? Like was Shaw our target? Doesn't look like it. Looks like we just wanted to kill people, and Shaw was in the wrong place at the wrong time."

"You shot a little girl, man. You killed a little girl."

"Well, and what about you? You didn't shoot *anybody*."

"I *tried*. I missed. I'm not like you. I don't do guns well."

"I'm wondering if I should tell Anders you pussed out. Tell him you didn't do your job. Maybe you're not really *with* us, Juan, is what I'm wondering if I should tell Anders."

"Dude—Crowder—I *told* Anders I don't do well with guns."

"You've been practicing, though, right? I've seen you practicing."

"Yeah, but—"

The car in front of me slows down, so I move into the left lane to pass.

"Hey!" Juan says, raising the gun a little. "No fuckin' funny business."

"I— I'm just passing." My voice cracks.

"Just watch it."

I don't think Juan could shoot me if he wanted to. But if he *didn't* want to . . . well, maybe that's what makes him dangerous.

"Get off at the next exit," the one in the back seat—Crowder—says.

I'm still in the left lane. It's going to be tough to get back into the right lane before we reach the exit. Traffic is getting tighter as it gets later in the morning. "I'm—"

"You nervous?" Juan says. He taps my leg with his gun. "You piss your pants?"

"I just— I need to get over. It's going to be— Give me a minute."

"Please don't miss the exit," Crowder says.

"You hear that? Don't you miss the fuckin' exit, you dumb fuck. You miss the exit, you fuckin' die."

"Juan, cool it, man."

I start to pull back into the right lane but this silver Mercedes Benz that was in my blind spot honks at me, lays on his horn. I swing back over to the left. A blue Buick that tried to close the gap I left beeps tersely and slows down, letting me over. The exit is only a little over a mile away. Between it and me are three lanes of traffic.

"The fuck?" Juan says.

"I'm— I just— I can't get over—"

"I said no fuckin' funny business! What are you trying to pull? What are you planning?"

"N-nothing. Nothing. I had to g— get over."

"You shoulda stayed in the right lane the whole time."

"You said—"

"You said. You said. Crowder, so help me, I wanna shoot this motherfucker right in the face."

"Juan, he's not trying anything. He's just trying to get over before the exit."

"He shouldn't have moved into the left lane in the first place. Why do you think he did that? He's trying to pull something. I don't know what, but he's trying to pull something on us."

My hands are trembling on the wheel. I check my mirrors but there's no room to get over. My signal is on, but this is L.A. Nobody cares if I miss my exit. Except for Juan and Crowder.

"This exit, please," Crowder says.

The exit is coming up. I can see it. I'm going to miss it.

"He said this exit!" Juan says. He jabs the gun into my leg, hard.

I'm going to miss it. I don't know what to do.

"Do you want to die? Do you want to fucking die?"

There's an orange Pontiac in the lane next to me now. Two other lanes of cars next to it.

"Fuck it. You're dead. You're trying to pull something over on me like I'm an idiot. I'm not a fuckin' idiot! You're dead!" Juan removes the gun from my leg and raises it, points it at my head, pulls back on the hammer. Even I know you don't have to pull back on the hammer, that that's just a movie thing.

"I'm not trying to pull anything!" I yell. "You said go the speed limit and I didn't know we'd be getting off so soon, you fucking idiot!" I push the gas as hard as I can and cut off the Pontiac and then tap the break pedal and slip in behind a dark green Audi and then slam the gas again and slide into the rightmost lane, between a semi and a Mini Cooper, and then into the exit lane and onto the ramp, just barely missing the steel barrier. My strawberry lemonade tumbles from the cup holder. In the rear view I see the Mini Cooper freak out and hit its brakes and the semi can't slow down and barrels into it and maybe even over it. There are the sounds of more crashes, but I'm already down the ramp.

I can tell in my periphery that Juan wants to squeeze the trigger. But his hand is shaking. This guy can't shoot a gun.

"Juan," Crowder says. "Put the gun down."

"He called me an idiot!"

"You are an idiot. Put the gun down. Now, you, please turn right and keep going."

I put on my right turn signal. I turn right. My pants are wet and my groin is starting already to itch.

"Juan, I said put the gun down. Somebody is going to see you. I've got this."

Juan sighs and lowers the gun. He doesn't point it back at my leg. "What are we gonna do with this guy?"

"We'll let Anders figure that out, okay?"

Juan grunts. "Okay. But if he says to kill him, I want to be the one to do it."

"Sure thing, buddy," Crowder says. Except I know for sure now that Juan won't ever be able to kill me or anyone. Crowder, on the other hand, I'm sure—I'm *positive*—has his own gun pointed at the back of my seat, and I know he'll shoot me if he thinks he has to, or if he's told to. Crowder doesn't lose his cool. I may have heard the story wrong but I'm pretty sure he's the sort of guy who kills little kids and doesn't bat an eye, is what it sounded like the story was.

KENNEDY

"You're telling me you were with him when he got shot?" Arnold asks, his mouth full of waffles I don't think he should be eating. He has a stack of them on the plate in front of him. Like five or six waffles all stacked up, slathered in butter and syrup and some sort of berry compote—blackberry or blueberry or some kind of berry.

"What? No. Did you even listen to me? I was with him last night. *Last night*. And, well—and this morning a little bit, too."

"This morning is when he got shot."

"Yeah, but—no. I was with him like *early* this morning."

Arnold takes a gulp from a large glass of orange juice, raspberry sherbet, and champagne. "And all night, too, is what it sounds like you're saying. You stayed the night."

"Yes. I stayed the night."

He wipes his hands with a napkin before picking up his knife and fork again. "How long have you two been fucking?"

I shrug. "I don't know. A few months. Six months."

"You sure you don't want some food or a drink or something?"

I gesture to my espresso. "I'm fine. I don't want to eat before the ceremony tonight. Maybe I'll munch something at one of the afterparties."

"You want more kratom?"

"No. Thanks. I probably shouldn't have taken what you already gave me. I feel . . . stimulated."

"Probably you *should* take more, but suit yourself. Listen— you should have told me about you and Beckett. He's—he was —a controversial figure sometimes. Some of the things he talked about didn't exactly line up with your political views."

"I don't *have* political views."

"You know what I mean. The views we set up for you. The image we've established. I'm not saying he was a bad guy, but if people knew you and him were sleeping together it could cause a lot of problems for you, socially speaking. Public image-wise."

"Arnold, he was *your* client too. Why would you be representing him if you thought he was so problematic."

"Oh, problematic isn't the . . . well, the problem. Problematic can be very lucrative. But it's in the same way that you, that"—and he does air quotes here, or what I've heard some people call bunny ears for some stupid reason —"Kennedy Thorne, are lucrative. Is lucrative. The persona, I mean, not the person. You need to keep your brand image very clear, very deliberate. You need to know where you're going and what people want to see from you, and then you need to do *that*, otherwise your audience is going to think you're inauthentic. Besides, if you two had told me you had a relationship, I could have made it work to my— to *your*—

advantage. To both of your advantages. There could have been some good spin there, some good opportunity. Had I known."

"We didn't really have a *relationship*. We were just fucking sometimes."

"Well—either way."

"Either way, Arnold, is that he's dead now. Beckett's dead. Aren't you kind of freaked out by that?"

"Sure, sure. But mostly I'm hungry. Right now, I mean. I mean, I'm gonna freak out later, I'm sure, like for real. But Beckett isn't my first dead client."

"That's comforting."

"He isn't even my youngest dead client."

"Doubly comforting."

"Kennedy—listen—" but then the waitress comes by with the side of bacon Arnold ordered after his waffles arrived. There are five pieces of bacon. He offers me one. I *am* hungry. I take one piece. I figure the fat will help keep me full until after tonight, and bacon *is* keto, right? So if I eat a piece it's not like I'm going to put on any weight.

"You were saying?" I say as I pop the piece in my mouth. It's salty and crunchy and suddenly I want more.

Arnold is silent for a moment.

"Arnold?"

"I'm just—I know I was going to say something. I just don't remember—Oh, yeah. What's your number one priority right now, Kennedy?"

"Um—being a great human? Making an impact? Connecting with others?"

"No no no. You're thinking too big, being too . . . sincere. And it's not a good look on you. I mean what's your biggest priority right now? That's what *priority* means. It means right now, what's the one thing you're devoting your time and attention to?"

I give this some thought. I take too long to answer.

"Winning an Oscar, Kennedy! Your number one priority is winning an—"

"An Oscar, winning an Oscar, right. Right. Sorry. I knew that."

"Jesus, Kennedy. Where is your head today? You went to J-Sean Laurentius's right, at least? You didn't fuck that up?"

"No. No, of course not. I went. I told you I did. I just left there. That's where I was when I saw the thing about—about Beckett."

"Forget about Beckett right now. Are you listening to me? Tonight is *the* biggest night of your career. Beckett is—was—a two-bit YouTuber with no actual goals or dreams. He didn't have any real purpose—"

"I wouldn't say that. He used to tell me about—"

"Kennedy, I was his manager. Do you know how many videos he put out? Like on a regular basis? His posting schedule?"

"I don't know. I didn't really watch them. Couple times a week?"

"Twice a month. *A month*. And I had to call him and get all the way on his back about it every time. The guy had no ambition, Kennedy. Just rich parents who set him up with a fat trust fund and who he didn't give a damn about. He thought all he had to do to be famous was livestream on Instagram and talk about whatever the fuck he wanted. Get high and just talk. But that's not you. You're the hardest working client I have. I've *ever* had. I mean that. You work really hard to craft your persona. I tell you to do something, and you do it. Now, granted, sometimes I get a little freaked out. You stress me out, Kennedy. You don't always text back and I don't know if you're where you're supposed to be and it gives me fucking anxiety attacks, but sure enough, you *are* where you're supposed to be. Ismi always tells me, 'Calm down, Arnold. I'm sure she's at J-Seans.' Or 'I'm sure she's at the senator's gala.' Or 'I'm sure she's at Jake Paul's studio right now filming that video.' And you know what? You are—every single time. I doubt you and I doubt you and I doubt you and I'm so stupid for doubting you every time I do."

It takes me a minute to realize that Arnold is crying. "Are you okay, Arnold?"

"I'm fine. I'm fine." He sniffles. "I'm fine. It's just—gosh. You're a really hard worker, okay, Kennedy? You're going to the Oscars with George Clooney tonight—"

"I'm not exactly going *with* him."

"But you're going to win Best Picture and you're going to stand up on stage with him. And he'll win Best Actor and you know why? Because he was in that scene with *you*. You deserve that award as much as he does."

"I don't get to go up on stage. You know that. My role wasn't that big."

"But it will be *like* you're up there on that stage."

I hadn't really thought of it that way. "You don't even know I'm going to win. That is, you don't know that *In My Eyes, Your Heart* is going to win. There are several great nominees."

"Well, and I didn't see any of them, but I know they're shit compared to yours. And you're going to get more film roles because of it. And soon, you're not going to be guest appearing on YouTube videos anymore. You'll be doing all film roles. And I don't mean Netflix Original Movies, either."

"I suppose," I say. "I'm just still . . . freaked out, I guess, about Beckett."

"That'll pass. I need you focused. I mean, *you* need you focused today. Listen, why don't you come over for the next few hours, before you have to go put the dress back on. You can smoke a joint with Ismi and me and just relax before the festivities."

"You know I don't do pot—"

"Hold that thought." Arnold pulls his phone out, looks at the screen. "Hey, listen, I need to take this. You good?"

"Sure," I say.

"Cool. Don't stress, okay? You're going to do great tonight. Big things are coming for you." He stands and puts the phone to his ear and says "Hello" and walks away, leaving me alone at the table.

ARNOLD

"Arnold Brewster?"

"This is he."

"Mr. Brewster—"

"Call me Arnold, please. Just Arnold. Everyone does."

"My name is Paul Gump. I'm a detective with the Los Angeles Police Department. I hope I'm not the first person to tell you this, but a client of yours, Beckett Shaw, was killed today."

"Yes, I heard. It's all over social media."

"That's what I assumed. We'd like to ask you a few questions about Mr. Shaw and the shooting, if you have the time."

"Why? I understand he wasn't the only one killed. Wasn't it just an accident? I don't mean an *accident*, but . . . wasn't he just a random victim."

"Probably. But we have some evidence that it may have been a targeted killing. That Mr. Shaw may have been the target. We'd just like to ask you a few questions about his recent activities."

"I can't say I know much about any activities, but of course I'd like to help."

"That's good to hear. Can you get down to the Northeast Community station within the next hour?"

"The . . . No, I'm sorry. My . . . wife, Esmeralda, is . . . quite sick today. I'm afraid I need to be there for her. I'm home all day and simply can't leave."

"I'm sorry to hear that. But I understand. My partner and I can stop by your home. You'll be there all day, of course, you said?"

"Yes, but—"

"Fantastic. Can you just confirm your address? We have some work to do here, so I can't say exactly when we'll be by, but you just sit tight."

"But—Listen, I have a very busy day. I want to help, but —"

"That's *very* good to hear, because we could really use your help, Mr. Brewster."

"Arnold, please."

"Of course, Arnold. Thank you for your cooperation. We'll be by as soon as we can. Won't take more than a few minutes."

"I—"

"You have a wonderful morning, Arnold. Hope your wife feels better. We'll see you soon."

I start to tell him that I'll have to maybe take Ismi to the doctor or something, but he's already clicked off. I don't know why I lied, except that I don't like talking to the police and it's a crazy day what with all my hopes being pinned on Kennedy and everything. The sun is not quite centered in the sky yet, and it's not even supposed to get above 75 degrees today, but I'm sweating and suddenly I'm finding it difficult to breathe.

"Ismi!" I call as I enter the foyer. "Ismi!"

"Arnold? What is it?" she asks as she rounds the corner from the media room. "Oh, my, you look—Did you eat sugar? How much sugar did you eat? You look hypertensive. Good god, Arnold."

Somewhere in the back of my mind I realize I left Kennedy just sitting there—I didn't pay the bill. "I'm fine. Dammit. I just need—"

She leads me to the living room and sits me on the couch. I have so much work to do. Time passes and she hands me a glass of water and two pills that I hope are Klonopin. I take them, chase them with the water.

"You can't keep doing this, Arnold. You know what the doctor said. You were doing so well. Just this morning you were doing so well—"

"I'm *fine*. Can you bring me my laptop? I think I left it outside."

She disappears and I stand up and take my shirt off. The shirt is drenched. Was that me? Did I sweat? Did I sweat that much?

"What are you doing?" Ismi asks when she returns. She sets my laptop on the couch.

"Looking for my pipe. Have you seen my pipe? I can't find my pipe."

"It's on the table next to you."

"Oh—yes, there it is. I need some Marigold's Gold."

"Why don't I just get you some more CBD drops?"

"No. I need the Marigold's. I need the THC, too."

"Okay, fine. I'll get it. I'll be right back."

Ismeralda rarely smokes. She'd rather be knitting or watching soap operas, I guess. She brings me the bud and I stuff it into the pipe and light it and inhale. I am instantly calmed by the perfect mixture of THC and CBD. I don't even remember what I was panicking about. "What?" I snap.

"Just . . . do you need anything else."

"No, thank you," I say. "I'm sorry. Thank you dear. You're wonderful. I just have some work to do now."

"Okay. Call for me if you need anything. I'm here."

"I appreciate that." As she walks away I half-remember something. "Oh, wait," I call.

"Yes?"

"How are you feeling?"

"Um—I'm fine."

"You're not sick or anything? Feverish?"

"No. I'm fine."

"Okay. I just thought you were— Hmm. Nevermind."

"Okay . . ."

"I love you," I say.

"I love you, too, Arnold."

When she's gone I lie back on the couch and take another hit of the pipe and then place my laptop on my belly and it's warm. I open my email client in one desktop instance and a web browser in another. I flip back and forth between answering email and browsing porn and I can't shake the feeling that there's something important I'm supposed to be doing today.

CARLOS

The air here in this place is cold and damp and gives me the chills. I have the sense of being in a dungeon or an old castle, or the dungeon of an old castle. When I was seven, before whatever it was that happened between my papa and my *abuela* that made them stop speaking to each other and left *Papá* to stubbornly fend for himself, make his own way, take care of his own family, just you watch what I can do it, we took a family trip to the ruins at Teotihuacán. While everyone was eating lunch, I snuck away and broke into one of the old apartments. I don't know how I got in, but it wasn't difficult, and I was a curious kid. I don't remember doing much there. I got scared and left and my family found me in the gift shop. I told them I'd been in the gift shop the whole time. My father hit me for running off. The coldness of those old ruins are what this place feels like.

I followed the rest of Crowder's instructions until we arrived in front of a beige building. On the outside, it looked normal. There were what looked like abandoned storefronts. There was a large parking lot, the kind you don't often see in Los Angeles. Crowder told me to park in front, next to a black van. I did. Juan asked whether he should shoot me now that I was done driving.

"I told you, we wait to see what Anders says."

Then Juan suggested they put a bag over my head.

"A bag?"

"Yeah, or something. Something so he don't see where we're taking him."

"But we're already here. He drove the whole way. He knows where we are."

"See, that's why we should just go ahead and *shoot* him, man."

In the end, Crowder removed his mask and told me to put it on, backwards. If I'm being honest, I was trembling as he told me this. I'm still trembling, because for all I know I'm being led to my execution, and no matter what happens the day won't end well. I didn't get a good look at Crowder's face even though he had his mask off. He was bearded, maybe, or lightly stubbled. His hair was either gray or brown. He was 40 years old or 25. The mask smells sweet like hair gel and musky like sweat.

Juan is telling Crowder how fucking hungry he is, man. His voice is echoing down the hallway. Crowder's gun is in my back and I go whichever way he tells me to go. "Right turn," he says.

I turn right and my shoulder bumps into a doorframe. "S-sorry," I mutter.

"Fuckin' funny business," Juan says and kicks my shin.

"Calm down, Juan," Crowder says.

I sense that we're in a room, no longer a hallway. "Sit here," Crowder says.

"And leave the mask on," Juan says.

I reach out and feel the arms of a chair. I sit. It's the kind of uncomfortable chair you'd find at the DMV.

"Sit tight. I'm going to go talk to Anders. Juan is going to look after you. Don't piss him off."

"Man, hurry up, man," Juan says. "I need me a fucking sandwich or something."

"Won't be a jiffy," Crowder says. "And I'll see if Anders has something you can eat." I hear a door open. Crowder's footsteps fade away.

I don't know whether I should talk, whether Juan expects me to talk, to keep him company. I sit silently for a time. Except then I realize I'm not silent. My fingers are tapping on the hard bony armrest. I am not tapping them; they are tapping of their own volition. Commanding them to stop takes a concerted effort. When they stop tapping, I can hear Juan's breathing. It's nasally. Like he's snoring while awake. Wheezing.

I think my heart rate has been running at 90, 95 percent of max for the last half hour. It's a wonder I'm not dead. I know of course that it hasn't actually been *that* high, that if it was I *would* be dead. I may have dropped out of school but I went long enough to know that extreme tachycardia is no joke. If anything, all I've had is moderate tachycardia. When I got to America and started school I wore a heart monitor for a week to get a sense of my baselines. It wasn't something a teacher required of us—I wasn't in school long enough to even remotely get into the depths of the cardio program—but rather something my academic advisor suggested I do. I think she could tell I wasn't actually into being a doctor, but she knew my situation and knew how important pleasing my father was to me, at least at the time, and so she said I should wear it, get in touch with my heart, figure out what makes it tick. Also I should do yoga, she said, and she handed me a business card, told me she had recently opened her own studio and could really use some students because growth was slow, and that's what she really wanted to do with her life, be a yoga teacher, maybe even for the rich and famous, not spend the rest of her life working at a university, advising students, even if the school did subsidize her housing and let her eat free meals on campus. Always she was dealing with whining students, people who had no idea what they were going to do with their life, no offense, and she just couldn't take it much longer, she just couldn't take it, she was a *spiritual* person. The heart rate monitor told me that I needed to work out more—my resting rate averaged in the low 90s—so I started walking on the treadmill and swimming in the campus pool, but the habits didn't really last. But based on the data I'd gathered about myself that week I know my heart rate has realistically probably been steadily up at around *at* least 160 since Juan and Crowder got in my car. Now, though, I can feel myself finally calming down. Maybe it's the hum of the florescent lights I *know* are out there. Maybe it's Juan's unhealthy breathing. Maybe it's that Crowder is out of the room. Maybe the Redbulls I had this morning are wearing off. Either way, I'm calming down, physically speaking, which is a good thing, except I have a hangover, and the headache comes rushing back—the heavy, itchy eyes, the dehydration. My mouth is dry. My pants are wet, I'm remembering, and my legs are itchy, more than uncomfortable. I can smell my urine now. I couldn't smell it before.

I hear music. I hear the sound of a cat mewing. I hear muttered voices. But all the sounds are . . . not *distant*, that's not the word. They're very nearby, but it's like they're coming from the inside of a tin can. Juan laughs, and I realize he's watching internet videos on his phone. My phone is still in my car, stuck to the windshield, inaccessible, useless. Juan's laugh is obnoxious, crude. I hate it. Suddenly I am filled with hatred. I've never felt this hatred before, except for my *papá* for never aspiring to be more than a bricklayer.

"Are you watching the hostage?"

It's Crowder. He's back. I didn't hear him coming. Hostage? Of course that's what I am. I'm not an actor—I'm a hostage. I suppose it's all I'll ever be now. I'm not going to make it to my audition.

"What? Dude, of course."

"It looks to me like you're watching your phone."

"Nah, man. I was—"

"I thought you were making sure he didn't get up to any 'funny business.'" There are air quotes around the words. I can hear them.

"Nah, of course. I was just—"

"Forget it. Here's a protein bar."

There's the sound of a wrapper being unwrapped. "Where's Anders?"

"Busy. He wants us to bring this guy back as soon as you're done eating."

"Okay, cool, cool. But yo, this ain't much man. You think I could get a sandwich or something? I'm *hungry*, man. It's gonna be a long day and I gotta like really eat something, you know?"

"Absolutely. That's just to hold you over. Anders says there's going to be a big lunch before the job."

"Ah—thanks, man."

"I got you. Now let's go."

Someone grabs my arms—I assume it's Crowder. "This way," he says. He prods me in the back, but I don't think with a gun this time. I move one foot in front of the other in the direction I think he's indicating. We walk maybe ten feet. Then Crowder, who's following behind me, says, "You can take the mask off, by the way."

"What?" Juan says. "Do you think that's a good idea, man? What if he sees something—?"

I'm wondering the same thing. If I take the mask off, I'll see something, which must mean they're planning on killing me no matter what I do.

"It's cool," Crowder says. "Anders says it's cool."

"I don't like it—Wait. Man, dude, wait—what are you—"

I reach up for the mask and it slides off my face concurrent with a sick wet cracking sound. The fabric clears my head and I turn around and there's Crowder, lightly bearded, standing behind Juan, who's slinking to the floor, eyes open but empty, staring at me but not staring at me, a protein bar wrapper at first clenched tight in his hand and then not. "Keep walking," Crowder says.

I turn back around. I walk forward. The interior of the building, I realize now, is not cold like I thought it was. In fact it's . . . nice. The walls are made of wood, the floor is carpeted, and the lighting is warm and gentle. This is not a dungeon. I could have sworn before that I was in a dungeon.

Who am I kidding? The audition I was supposed to go to today was for a soap commercial. What role could any casting director ever find for me in a soap commercial?

"That door on the left."

I open the door and walk in, unprepared to meet my fate. My chest hurts. There are ten or so men in the room—I can't exactly count right now. They're standing or sitting around a heavy oak table. Some are working at laptops. Others are eating. In the middle of the table are two carafes and two plates of croissant sandwiches. One of the men looks up from his laptop. He's white, maybe in his early thirties. He has a beard nicer than I could ever grow. "Howdy," he says. He looks behind me. "Juan?"

"In the hallway," Crowder answers. "Someone should move him, though. I can do it."

"No, you stay here. Vickers, you do it."

One of the guys whose eating gets up, dabs a napkin at the corner of his mouth. "On it."

"Sorry," Crowder says to him. "I did it clean, though. There's no blood or anything. Just the body."

"Cool," Vickers says. "Probably still crapped his pants, though."

"Shame, really," says another guy.

The first guy, with the beautiful beard, shrugs. "Necessary, though. Sounds like Juan was a liability. Crowder, hungry?"

"Very."

The guy looks at me. "You hungry?"

"I . . . um . . ."

"It's not a trick question. Grab a sandwich. There's coffee. I'm Anders. Tell me: are you angry? Are you outraged? If you're outraged, we could really use your help."

KEELY

J-Sean is upstairs having sex with Stuart. I wonder for a moment what that means, what that looks like. Are they just blowing each other, or are they like really fucking? I know J-Sean keeps a tub of coconut oil on the nightstand by his bed. They're being quiet. You can't hear them. But I know they're having sex because that's what I'd be doing right now if I was Stuart: having sex with J-Sean. Hell, probably if I was J-Sean I'd be having sex with Stuart, even though I can't stand the guy. Something about him . . . he just doesn't seem trustworthy. There's a feeling I have that he's taking advantage of J-Sean, but I can't put together how. J-Sean is very successful, sure, has a lot of money and a solid amount of a certain kind of fame, but Stuart isn't doing so bad either. A piece of his sold to Gigi Hadid for like a hundred grand three months ago. I know because she posted about it on Instagram and so did he. I picture J-Sean going down on Stuart. I picture Stuart going down on J-Sean. I picture J-Sean fucking Stuart in the ass and I'm a little jealous. I'm self-aware enough to recognize that I'm a little jealous. I've been working with my therapist on self-awareness. It's been a particular focus of our sessions the last couple months. I'm pretty sure Stuart is bi. Leilani told me last week when she was pretty drunk that she slept with him, also when she was pretty drunk. I'm certain J-Sean doesn't know, but I'm not certain whether he'd care. J-Sean is as gay as they come, though, which makes me sad. Although I did hear a rumor he made out with Miley Cyrus once, but that's Miley Cyrus.

Leilani and Maurice are in the workshop making alterations to Kennedy Thorne's dress. Fuck, they're probably making out right now, too. Everybody is getting some but me, it seems. I haven't had sex since last week. I've just been too busy.

"You're not going to believe this, but I have an email from Bono's rep saying he's interested in collaborating with J-Sean on some charity thing," Renalda says to me. I jump. I didn't hear her approach. She's holding an iPad and pointing to it with her other hand.

"Who's Bono?" I ask.

"Who's . . . He's the singer for U2."

"YouTube?"

"No, *U2*."

"I don't know who that is," I say.

"U2? They're one of the most famous bands of all time."

"Since when?"

"I don't know—like the 80s."

"Well that explains it. Let me see. It's probably a scam, and if it isn't, I doubt this Bono is someone J-Sean is going to want to waste his time with."

Renalda hands me the tablet and as she does I can't help but examine her. Her hair. Her face. Her upper body. She's not having sex right now either, I realize.

"Do you have a boyfriend?" I ask.

"Yeah," she says, maybe a little shyly. "But he's back in Ohio."

"He didn't want to move to California?"

"He's at OSU on a football scholarship. I miss him."

I examine the email on the iPad. "When was the last time you saw him?"

"A couple month ago, right before I came out here. At the end of his winter break. We did Christmas with his family in Akron . . ."

"I don't know where that is."

"Oh—right. It's northeastern Ohio. It's where I grew up —"

I hand the iPad back to her. "This is fake," I say. I don't tell her that her boyfriend is definitely cheating on her. She's a sweet girl. I used to be a sweet girl like her, before I grew up.

"I don't think it is. Look at the address. And there's a phone—"

"You're new," I say. "We get scam emails like this all the time. I didn't recognize some of them when I first started either. You'll learn. Besides, I still don't know who Bono even is. Neither does J-Sean."

I say this last part as I walk away, over to the wet bar. I'm torn between a gin and juice or an espresso. Renalda reminds me a lot of me when I started working for J-Sean. She really does. I came down from Shasta and had never experienced the big city before. But I met J-Sean's old assistant at a party and showed her some sketches on my phone and she got me an internship with J-Sean. I was a baby. I'd probably still be that baby, but then his old assistant killed herself and J-Sean decided he liked me and gave me the promotion. I settle on a hazelnut latte from the Keurig.

While I wait for it to brew I check my phone.

There's a text . . . from my mom. She says she hasn't heard from me in a while and just wants to check in. I ignore it. I'll respond later. I will, really—as long as I remember.

There's a Snap from this Tinder date I went out with two nights ago. I open it. Gross. It's a picture of his penis, and it's not even an attractive penis. It's short and stumpy and I wish more guys would trim their pubes back. I shouldn't have gone on the date in the first place. I should know by now that any guy who's still using Tinder is *not* someone you want to go on a date or have sex with. I block him.

There's a comment on one of my Instagram posts. I open it. Nevermind. It's not even a recent post. It's this post from over a month ago, some travel agency saying they love my pics and will I please check out their page. Come to think of it, I don't remember ever giving the Tinder guy my Snapchat. I guess I must have, though. I should know by now that any guy who's still using Snapchat just wants to send dick pics or follow porn stars.

I'm in this group message thread with a bunch of girls I grew up with. There are five new messages in there. Four of them are GIFs. I send a winky face. I briefly feel guilty about this one girl, Tiana, because she's not in the thread anymore.

She got a new phone and the messages turned green, and once we realized it was Tiana making the messages turn green, Evelyn said we should start another thread without her, which we did.

The Keurig gurgles like a man who's been shot in the throat. I pick up my mug. I take a sip. Discreetly, I add a splash of amaretto.

"Mornin' love." Stuart is next to me at the wet bar. He pulls a coffee mug off the self and puts it in the Keurig.

"Hey," I say. "It's like almost noon."

"Still mornin' though, innit?" he says. He picks a black coffee pod.

I shrug. He's wearing a silk robe, belted at the waist, that comes down to just above his knees. His legs are tan and only a little hairy. His chest is smooth. His eyes are red from whatever he got high on last night. I wonder whether he's wearing underwear. "I've been up since five," I say.

"You're cute," he replies, as he fills a large glass with water. He turns around and leans against the bar as he drinks it, surveys the studio. "You lot gettin' up to today? Lotsa hard work it looks like, yeah?"

I roll my eyes but also I want him. "We have a big client we're working with today. She's going to the Oscars tonight and we're the dress. I'm surprised J-Sean didn't tell you."

He shrugs. "Maybe he did. She here? Who is it? Cate Blanchett? Natalie Portman?"

"Well—no. This other girl. She's not really famous or anything."

"Ah, damn. Well, someday, yeah? And you can say you knew her first."

"Yeah, maybe—" I say. Although I doubt it. "So where's J-Sean?"

"He's just takin' a shower, I fink. He was in a right mood this morning, wasn't he?"

"You're telling me."

"Yeah, well, I think I calmed him down some for ya, love." He pats me on the shoulder and winks and that's harassment, isn't it? But also it turns me on. Stuart has this way of being creepy and sleazy and charming all at once. I'm 80 percent sure his accent isn't real.

I see Leilani walking toward me with what looks like a question on her face. I leave Stuart behind and meet her half way. "What's up?" I ask.

"We have a . . . small problem."

"Uh oh?"

"Maurice was making an adjustment to the back of the dress, down where the client's back will be, and—well, fuck, can you come into the workshop for a sec?"

I don't like the sound of this. My eyes float toward the ceiling, as if I'm hoping they can see through it and check that J-Sean won't be down for a while.

In the workshop, I at first can't tell what's going on. Maurice is there, and he's holding his arm up, saying, "Oh shit oh shit oh shit."

"Can we turn the lights up?"

"But then . . ."

I understand what Leilani is afraid of. If we turn the lights up, then whatever's happening in here will be visible through the glass, out in the studio. "Just a little," I say. "Alexa, turn up the lights."

The warm workshop lights get brighter, and I understand now. Well, I don't understand, but I see. "What the hell happened?"

There's blood dripping down the arm that Maurice is holding high. It's originating from somewhere on his hand, flowing down his arm, and onto the the drafting table, onto the dress, which is an off-white dress. Except now parts of it are not off-white. Parts of it are the red of the carpet it's meant to be worn on.

"I— I— I—" Maurice says. He runs his hand across his face, through his bleached hair. Now there's blood in his hair and on his face. "Fuck fuck fuck."

"Maurice was making an adjustment. Here"—Leilani points to a particularly bloody part of the dress, near the waist —"and he—"

"There was a—a pin. I didn't see the pin." Maurice seems to be gasping for breath.

I'm calm. I know that soon I may not be calm, but right now I'm calm as I piece together the story. "Okay, so you stabbed yourself with the pin. That happens all the time." I can't even count the number of times I've done it myself. It hurts, it sucks, but it's not a big deal. We keep bottles of color-safe bleach around the workshop for that reason—it's easy to remove a pin-prick's worth of blood. "But there's way too much blood for that . . ."

"Way too much blood," Maurice says. "*Way* too much!"

"Alexa, turn the lights back down," I say. "I don't understand. What happened?"

"The scissors . . ."

"He was cutting a thread," Leilani says.

"Okay . . ."

"With kitchen shears."

"*What?* Why?"

"He thought it was funny."

"And then he—?"

"I cut my finger off!"

"Fuck," I say. "Turn the light back on."

"It's just the tip," Leilani says, as she raises the dimmer switch manually.

"There," I say. "No brighter." I look toward the window. It doesn't appear that anyone has noticed that anything is wrong in here. Stuart is talking to Renalda, making a jacking-off motion. She seems either disgusted or embarrassed.

"KEELY!"

Fuck. That's J-Sean. I see him come down the stairs.

"Fuck," I say. "Okay. Lights down again. Fix the dress."

"I don't know that we can."

"Find a way. ASAP."

"What about my finger?" says Maurice, whose breathing is becoming more steady. "Oh my god."

"Dress first," I say. "And you shouldn't have been such an idiot. Wrap your hand up. And I mean wrap it up really well, so that you don't keep fucking bleeding all over everything, and then you fix this fucking dress—"

"KEELY!"

Fuck. "I'm here!" I call out as I leave the workshop. J-Sean is shirtless and damp. He's holding his phone in one hand. He sees me. He starts to storm over. I move fast and close the distance, keeping him as far from the workshop as possible. "What's wrong?"

"Look," he says. He thrusts his phone into my face.

I reach out to take it from him. He jerks his hand back. "J-Sean, I can't see anything. Your screen turned off."

He glances at his phone. "Ugh. Sorry. Here. Just look."

He surrenders the phone to me. It's just his Instagram timeline. "Should I be scrolling?" I ask.

"Scroll," he says.

I scroll. "I'm sorry . . . I don't know what I'm supposed to be seeing . . ."

"It's what you're *not* seeing!"

I realize all the photos I'm looking at are of J-Sean. J-Sean and Wiz Khalifa. J-Sean and Miley Cyrus. J-Sean and Khloe Kardashian. J-Sean and Jimmy Fallon (I don't remember when that one could have possibly been taken). J-Sean and Bernie Sanders. J-Sean and Terry Crews. J-Sean and Selma Hayek—

"See?" he says.

I don't. I scroll back to the top. I'm not looking at J-Sean's timeline. I'm looking at the part of his profile that displays all the photos he's been tagged in. "Shit—" I start to say.

"She still hasn't posted the photo!"

"Maybe she just forgot to tag you." I hand his phone back to him. I pull out my phone, unlock it with my face, open the

app, type in her name. Her last photo is some shitty cold brew
—I've tried it—and sparkling water. Fuck.

"Where's Leilani?" J-Sean says. "Leilani! Leilani!"

"She busy with—"

"LEILANI!"

"Here. I'm here. What's up, boss man?" She's poking her
head out of the workshop door. I can't tell for sure, but I think
there might be blood on her face.

"The Thorne dress—" J-Sean says.

"Yeah, it's great! It's coming along great. Almost done."

"Cancel it."

"What—?"

"J-Sean—" I say.

"Cancel. It."

"J-Sean, we need—"

"CANCEL IT!"

Leilani looks at me. I jerk my head to the side. She raises
an eyebrow. She might be shrugging but I can't tell for sure
because only her head is visible. I shake my head.

"Goddammit," Maurice yells from inside the workshop.

"What's that?" J-Sean asks.

"Nothing," Leilani says. "It's . . . nothing. We're all good in
here."

"Well put the fucking dress away. Burn it or something."

"Burn—?"

"Just get rid of it. I'm sick of bending over backwards for
a fucking cunt that can't even give me some fucking credit.
That bitch is *cancelled*."

"Of course," Leilani says. "Got it. On it." She disappears back into the workshop, closing the door behind her.

"J-Sean, look—" I start to say, but he's storming back up the stairs.

I look at Stuart. "A little help?"

He raises his wrist as if he's wearing a watch. "I have a meeting in Chinatown in a half hour, love."

Probably with his opium dealer or something.

"Fuck you," I say. He shrugs, raises his coffee as if toasting me. I send Kennedy Thorne a text. As I head up the stairs after J-Sean I wonder whether I should just kill myself.

KENNEDY

I'm walking down Melrose Avenue listening to a podcast on my AirPods when my phone starts to ring. Ring isn't the right word, is it? Ringtone doesn't make any sense. The tone of a ring, I realize now, all of a sudden, shocked I've never had the thought before, is a *ring*. But mine is the song "Old Town Road" by Lil Nas X featuring Billy Ray Cyrus, which is absolutely nothing like a ring. "Old Town Road" interrupts Joe Rogan, who's talking to Joey Diaz, who, when I can understand what he's talking about, I think is funny and who I saw at The Comedy Store once . . . with Beckett. Beckett often told me that a big life goal of his was to be on Joe Rogan's podcast. "To talk about what?" I asked him. "I dunno. You know—to just . . . bullshit and shit."

I reach up with my left hand to double tap the AirPod and take the call. The first time I double tap it doesn't work, the podcast keeps playing, so I try again. The second time I double tap, on the second tap, the earpiece falls out of my ear and gets caught in the collar of my sweater. I reach for it there and it falls to the ground. "Old Town Road" is still playing in my right ear, but then it stops. "Hello?" I say, but there's no answer. I pick up my AirPod. I resume walking.

I don't have a destination in mind.

As we were coming out of The Comedy Store Beckett asked me why I like Joe Rogan and Joey Diaz if I don't smoke pot. I told him I didn't know what he meant. He said, "Those guys are high, like, all the time. You know that, right? They're always super fucking high."

"They are?"

"Fuck yeah, they are. That thing Joey Diaz just said about pedophiles in Thailand—you just don't say stuff like that if you're not high. And you don't laugh at stuff like that if you're not high either."

"Are you high right now?"

"Right now? Probably not. But I ate a 15 milligram edible before we went in there. It always makes things funnier."

"Well, I'm not high, and I thought he was funny. They were all funny, except the blonde girl."

"I though she was funny. I thought the thing about getting her pubes stuck in her zipper was funny."

"Yeah, well I didn't."

"Probably because you wax."

I shrugged.

"You really should try at least an edible some time."

"I don't touch substances." Anymore.

"So you say, but I've seen you drink alcohol. And CBD—"

"CBD isn't psychoactive."

"So everyone says. But alcohol definitely is—"

"I don't get drunk."

"I've seen you drunk."

"I don't get drunk."

"Well, and anyway, what do you call that?" he asked as I took a hit of my Juul.

I handed it to him. "It just tastes good."

He took a hit himself and gave it back to me. "You may not do 'drugs,' Kennedy, but you're such a stoner."

"What? No I'm not."

He laughed and put his arm around me. "You're such a stoner and you don't even know it."

"I'm *not* a stoner."

"You don't have to get high to be a stoner."

"I'm not a stoner."

He kissed me on the forehead. Beckett was taller than me by nearly a foot, which always gave him such tender access to my forehead. "Stoner, stoner, stoner," he said gently. This was all just last December. Just a couple months ago. I remember the night was cool, and his arm around me felt reassuring. His lips on my head were warm. "Kennedy—" he said, gently, but I told him not to say anything else. I didn't want to hear it, and I knew he'd regret saying it, some day.

My phone rings again. I double tap the AirPod and it works this time, but I can't seem to say hello.

"Hello," says the voice in my ear. "Kennedy Thorne?" The voice sounds familiar, but I can't even try to place it. I seem to have lost myself.

PAUL

"Miss Thorne?" I say again. "Miss Thorne?"

I put my phone down and Adeline looks at me from across the office and says, "What happened, Paul?"

"I don't know," I say. "She definitely answered the phone. I thought I heard her mumble 'what' or something like it, but maybe not. Either way she didn't really say anything."

"You're sure it was her?"

"I'm sure it was her phone I called, if that's what you mean. I'm not an idiot."

"You're kind of an idiot, Paul."

"Well I didn't dial the wrong number. Couldn't tell you whether she was the one that answered."

Adeline chews on her pen. "She could be in danger."

"Didn't sound like it. All I heard was cars. Birds."

"You could hear birds over the sound of cars?"

"I said I heard birds."

"What kind of birds?"

"What kind of birds? I don't know what kind of birds." I sit and put my feet up on my desk.

"She could be in danger."

"Don't think so," I say.

"Maybe she knows something, though."

"Probably the one who did it."

"What? You serious?"

I shrug. "Could be."

"You think a twenty-three-year-old woman nominated for an Oscar tonight—"

"She's not nominated. Her movie is."

"Still. A woman who's attending the Oscars tonight and who was in a movie that will probably win an Oscar—"

"Entertainment Tonight says it won't. Says that Meryl Streep one is way more likely."

"Paul. So help me."

I shrug. "Just what they say." I point to my computer monitor, where I have the article pulled up.

"Okay. Whatever. But you seriously think a woman who's attending the Oscars—whose career dreams are coming true tonight—walked into a coffee shop this morning and killed a little girl."

I shrug. "Could be."

"You're so obtuse, Paul."

I don't know what obtuse means, so I open my drawer and pull out the sandwich my wife made me for lunch. "All I'm saying is maybe they had a—a what-do-you-call-it—a lovers' quarrel. They were seen leaving the senator's fundraiser together last night. Maybe something went bad after."

"We don't even know whether they were sleeping together."

"If," I tell her.

"What?"

I'm chewing a bite of my sandwich now so I have to take a second to swallow. "If," I say. "I think you mean we don't know *if* they were sleeping together."

"Oh my god," Adeline says. "Oh my god. I'm going to kill myself. It's *whether*, Paul. For fuck's sake."

"Don't think so," I say. I take another bite. "Plus she always goes to that coffee shop. You saw her Instagram posts."

"It *is* an interesting connection. Although, like the owner said, she got paid to do that. Did you get ahold of Thorne's manager?"

"Oh, fuck." I open my drawer again and pull out a can of V8 juice. I open it.

"'Fuck' what? What is it?"

I take a smallish bite of my sandwich and wash it down with a gulp of V8.

"Paul. 'Oh fuck' what? What is it?"

"No, nothing. I just forgot to call the manager."

"Oh for—"

"What? I'll call after I eat. I'm starving."

"Paul. Her manager is *his* manager. You didn't think maybe calling him was a priority—"

I laugh.

"What is it, Paul? What the fuck is it?"

"I'm fucking with you," I say. "I called him back at the coffee shop."

"What? What the fuck, Paul?"

"You shoulda seen the look on your face."

"Fuck you, Paul."

"It was hysterical."

"Is he coming down to the station or not?"

"Coming down? No, no. We need to go over there. Something about his kid is sick or something. He can't get out of the house."

"*What?* Then why did we come back to the station?"

"My sandwich was here. I was hungry. It was nearly lunch time."

"For fuck sake, Paul. That's it. I'm making sure you get taken off this case—fuck, off the force once this day is over." She picks up her keys and heads for the door.

"I'll follow you over there!" I call after her. I take another bite of my sandwich. It's not that I don't care about the case. I just think Adeline takes her job too seriously sometimes. All this death—it gets to a detective. I try hard not to let it.

CARLOS

I'm scared. I'm eating a croissant sandwich with American cheese and turkey and lettuce and tomatoes and some kind of garlicky aioli and I'm scared. This guy Anders is at the head of the table, standing in front of a white board, going over some sort of plan. I'm drinking coffee. There's coffee on the table. I poured myself a mug. Ever since I came to America I haven't been able to stop drinking coffee. I drink at least three cups a day, but some days, most days, I drink four, five, six cups of coffee. Not to mention the Red Bulls and Monsters and Rockstars and other energy drinks. Even Starbucks makes an energy drink. It's disgusting, but sometimes I buy it. You can't drive Uber if you aren't caffeinated. You just can't. You simply can't. I should have slept more last night. I shouldn't have gone to that party. Or that other party. I shouldn't have done that cocaine. My heart is going to explode today I just know it. This is my second sandwich. I am going to need a third.

Crowder is eating sandwiches too. He's no longer pointing his gun at me.

Anders has a little projector connected to his laptop. Just a little projector, one of those pocket ones that costs a couple hundred bucks and that you can fit in your bag, probably even in your pocket if you had a big pocket. It's pointed at the whiteboard so that on the whiteboard is this rectangle mirroring the contents of Anders' laptop screen. My mama's probably never seen one of these projectors. My papa definitely hasn't. I bet *Abuela* has, in Mexico City. She's such a hip lady. She had a smartphone before I did.

The projection of Anders' laptop screen has all these tweets scrolling by. It's somebody's twitter feed. Or maybe it's Anders' timeline and these are people he follows? I don't know. I don't use Twitter. I use Snapchat. Just Snapchat.

Anders says, "And here we have more progressive pandering bullshit. Do you think Alyssa Milano actually believes this shit?"

"Doubt it!" one of the guys at the table yells. It's all guys at the table. It's all white guys at the table, except for me.

"Damn right," Anders says.

Everyone laughs. I don't understand why they're laughing. I really don't. I want to cry. My left hand is on the table and I'm tapping the table with my fingertips.

"Who do they think we are?" Anders says.

"Yeah!" says another guy.

"Do they think we're stupid? Do they think we're just nobodies, with no opinions, no thoughts, no—fuck—no *feelings*?"

"Fuck them!" says another guy.

"Fuck them," says Anders.

A cry of "fuck them" erupts around the table. "Fuck them," I mutter. I reach for another sandwich. Fuck who—I don't understand.

"Did you guys hear about this?" Anders says, clicking around on his laptop. "Look at this." He pulls up some sort of news story. "This guy has the best free-throw record in recorded high school basketball history, gets a scholarship offer to play at a bunch of schools. Duke, Kentucky, Syracuse . . . here in L.A. Guy takes Duke. Signs the deal with Duke. This all happened just yesterday. Kid doesn't graduate high school for another four months but he knows where he's going to college . . . and for free too. How many colleges did you apply to?"

"Seven," one guy says.

"Five," says another.

"I'm Canadian," Crowder says. Everyone laughs.

Anders says, "I applied to fifteen universities. *Fif-fucking-teen*. And two accepted me, and I had to take out a hundred grand in student loans. So I could get a fucking liberal arts degree, a fucking art history degree. Damn, boys. If only I could have thrown a *ball* into a *loop* with a *net on it*."

There are chuckles, but not sustained laughter. "I like basketball," one guy mutters.

"Crowder, take care of this guy," Anders says. Crowder mimics reaching for his gun. Pew, he mouths.

Everyone laughs, this time hard.

"Joking," Anders says. "I like basketball too, when it isn't a tool of the liberal elite. A tool of the pedophiles and the fake news media machine."

"Here," one guy says, and raises his mug.

"Football's way better," says another guy.

"'Cept when they're disrespectin' our flag," says another."

"Here!" says the first guy. He raises his mug again.

"Here here," says Anders. Anders picks up a water glass and holds it high.

Everyone is raising their mugs or glasses. I find that I am too. Everyone is laughing. Not at me—no one's paying attention to me—but at the fact that our glasses are raised. There's a joke I'm missing here. An irony or a subtext. Something is going over my head. My papa used to tell jokes and I never got them. Always they'd go over my head. *Maldito idioto,* my father would say when I'd laugh. You don't have to pretend, you dumb kid.

The laughter dies down, and Anders says, "But seriously. How many of you are still drowning in student debt?"

Every hand goes up. I find mine going halfway up, compelled by a fear of what will happen if it doesn't.

"Carlos," Anders says.

I look around. Apparently I am the only Carlos in the room. "Y-yes?"

"What's your story? How much student debt do you have?"

"I . . . Like 5,000 dollars."

There are a couple gasps.

"Just five grand? Huh. How'd that happen?"

"I . . . dropped out."

"Ah," Anders says. "He dropped out."

Everyone claps.

"Anyway," Anders says, "We all worked really hard to get our degrees. And I don't know about the rest of you, but I can't even get more than 20 thousand followers on Instagram. Fat fucking lot of good college did me. I had to learn how to trade bitcoin all by myself—"

One guy cheers loudly for bitcoin.

"—and I had good grades, too. Not great, but good. But remember Felicity Huffman? She pays a guy like 15 grand to fake her kid's test scores, she gets two weeks in prison and a $30,000 fine. Thirty grand. Did the judge miss the part where that's only twice what she'd already paid to get her kid into college? So, what, it costs her 45 thousand, total? Big whoop for her, right?"

One guy boos. Another guy boos. I wish I could keep track of which guy is which when they boo or cheer or applaud or laugh, but they're just all blending together for me—except for Crowder, who's silent most of the time, and Vickers, who's returned from doing whatever he did with Juan.

"Fucking cunt," one of the two booers says.

"Now now," says Anders, "that's not a nice word. But, yes, I tend to agree."

A smattering of applause.

"But look at this." Anders does some stuff to his computer. A Twitter account comes up on the whiteboard. "Huffman's back on Twitter, telling the world how much she hates our president."

"Boo," says one of the guys who booed before—I think.

I notice that my foot is tapping rapidly against my leg. I make a conscious effort to hold it still.

"Carlos," Anders says. "Who'd you vote for?"

I don't know why he's talking to me again. I don't want him to be talking to me again. "W-what?"

"Did you vote for Hillary? I bet you didn't vote for Hillary."

I shake my head.

"You didn't?"

"N-no," I stammer. "I didn't."

"Good man," Anders says. "Doesn't matter who you *did* vote for, honestly, just who you didn't."

"I guess so."

"Anyway," Anders claps his hands together. "We've got some swamp draining to do this evening, gentleman. You all ready?"

"Yeah!" the guys, except for Crowder, say in unison.

"Carlos, I'm down a man, as you know. And I'm—well, I'm very sad about that, but it can't be helped. But if you're interested, I think you'd make a great part of our team tonight."

"I—"

"Listen—you wanna leave, you can leave. You can walk right out that door. No hard feelings. But we're about to get into some deep shit now. Some real deep hardcore planning. We got a gap in that plan now, a hole, and we could really use you there. But you don't have to do it. Be a shame if you didn't —but we could move some guys around. But if you're gonna stick around, you've got to stick around. No going back after this. I couldn't have that."

Every guy is looking at me. I don't make eye contact with any of them. But then I make eye contact with Crowder, and I know, I *know*, that if I walk out of this room I'm a dead man, same as Juan.

So—"I'm with you guys," I manage to croak.

ADELINE

As I approach the house on West Rosewood something starts to buzz in the back of my brain. I'm not sure what to make of it, but it's not unlike this thing that happens sometimes when I'm going into a dangerous situation. When I know my life will be in danger if I don't stay alert, react quickly, keep a level head. In those situations—entering a dark alley or searching for a missing person in a crack den—I might draw a weapon. Probably not my gun, because I try very hard to draw my gun as little as possible, because I'm a Buddhist and I don't want to kill anyone, but my taser or my baton. I fight very well with my baton. Sometimes I don't draw a weapon—don't have time—but just hold my hands out in front of my body loosely, ready.

This feeling I have right now isn't exactly like that. It's close, and maybe there's danger there, but the danger doesn't feel immediate. Something is just . . . off here. Like something is dying, not physically, but spiritually, inside this house. I cross my right hand over my body and touch my firearm, just to imprint onto my brain that it's there in case my instincts have failed me. I ring the doorbell.

The door tone is a bell rendition of "Straight Outta Compton" by N.W.A. I know that doesn't sound possible, and it takes me a couple seconds to recognize it, but that's what it is.

Only a little bit past noon and it's been a day, let me tell you. Some days are like this. Sometimes, as the kids say, or as Paul says, it really do be that way. I can't connect with the kids. They tell me I'm a millennial, but even millennials are the outdated ones now, I've come to understand. Thirty-four and I feel even older most days, when I'm dealing with Paul's ignoramity or my daughter, Jessie, is upset that there's no time to watch an episode of *Masha and the Bear* on Netflix before heading off to daycare—like she was this morning. It's my fault she didn't have time. I woke at 5 like I always do, but she wasn't up like she usually is. I peeked in on her and saw she was still fast asleep and decided to let her sleep as much as she needed. I gently closed her door and went back to my room. I masturbated for ten minutes, and then I spent the rest of the hour on the cushion. I rarely get to spend time on the cushion these days, since Eva died. Eva would always watch Jessie for me, every morning, so I could get in 15, 20, 30 minutes on a good day. Eva was a blessing. She was a wonderful mother, an unmatchable wife. These days I try to close my eyes for five minutes here or there, like if Paul goes to the bathroom. Sometimes Paul eats these sausage rolls from the truck across the street for lunch and I know I might get a solid 15 minutes alone at my desk to focus on the breath. I'm grateful for those days. I woke Jessie and made her breakfast and we sang a song together, but there was no time to watch *Masha and the Bear*.

I ring the doorbell again. I knock twice for good measure. I wonder briefly whether the knocking was a manifestation of impatience. I check in. It wasn't, I decide. It was appropriate, the knocking, to the situation.

A woman opens the front door. Hispanic. A little plump. A decade or so older than me. Kind eyes. "Can I help you? Is everything okay? Is something wrong?"

I'm a little irritated that Arnold Brewster didn't tell his housekeeper or his maid or whoever this woman is that the police would be stopping by. "Is Mr. Brewster available?" I ask. "I'm here to ask a few questions about a client of his. He should be expecting me." It occurs to me that Paul could have been lying and never called. It's possible Mr. Brewster has no reason to expect me.

The woman eyes me warily. I think it's warily. Finally she says, "Arnold isn't feeling very well today."

"That's odd," I say. "He told us his kid wasn't feeling very well, but he said nothing about himself."

"What?" the woman says. "We don't have any children."

Fuck. I now know two things: Somebody's lying—either Paul or Arnold Brewster—and this woman is not Paul's housekeeper. I feel guilt at having made the latter assumption. "May I come in."

"Come in. Come in. Can I get you something to drink?"

"That's not necessary."

"Then wait here, please. I'll go check on Arnold."

Mrs. Brewster disappears through an archway off the foyer. The foyer is very white. There's a waist-high vase next to the door with an umbrella in it. Two large paintings on the walls. I don't recognize the artist, but they appear to be by the same person. They're . . . contemporary. They're composed of shapes and colors that as far as I can tell aren't intended to represent anything in reality. They're not prints, but real paintings. Possibly the Brewsters paid a great deal for them. Possibly they paid next to nothing.

On a small table is a photograph of Mrs. Brewster and a man I presume to be Arnold Brewster. Again, I shouldn't make assumptions, but I think this is a safe one. There's a key fob on the table—and a leather wallet, a pocket knife, and a vape pen.

Mrs. Brewster reappears. "Arnold is available. He's in here. Follow me. You sure I can't get you something to drink?"

I follow her through the archway, down a narrow but short hallway. Through another archway. Arnold Brewster is sitting on the couch.

"Mr. Brewster, I'm Detective—"

"Arnold, please. Call me Arnold."

"Of course, Arnold. Arnold, my partner called you about your client, Beckett Shaw? I have few questions about him."

"I don't know how much I can be of help. I told your partner I don't know how much I can help."

"Of course, I understand. But you'd be surprised—sometimes the littlest details—we'd just like to get to the bottom of his death."

"Someone died?" Mrs. Brewster says.

"Ismi! Don't worry about it."

"I'm afraid so," I say.

"For god's sake, Arnold. Why didn't you say something?"

"Ismi! What did I—? Just go make us some coffee."

"That's not necessary—"

"Would you like some coffee?" Mrs. Brewster asks. "Or some water. We have sparkling water."

"Sparkling water would be great," I say.

"You don't want some coffee," Arnold says. "She can make coffee."

"I don't drink caffeine."

"We have herbal tea."

"Water is fine."

"I need coffee, Ismi. Coffee for me, water for the detective."

"You're not supposed to have the caffeine either—"

"Ismi!"

Mrs. Brewster smiles at me and leaves the room via a second archway.

"She means well," Mr. Brewster—Arnold—says.

"Mr. Brewster—"

"Arnold."

"Arnold. We believe it's quite possible your client, Beckett Shaw, was the victim of a targeted killing—"

"An assassination."

"Well—no, because he wasn't—. Anyway, someone, we think, tried to kill him, and they succeeded, and they killed a little girl in the process—"

"Oh my god," Mrs. Brewster says. She's returned with a glass of sparkling water.

"Ismi! What the fuck?"

"Thank you," I say, taking the water.

"It's from the SodaStream. I didn't know if you wanted any flavoring. We have cherry and raspberry and this hazelnut that I don't actually like—"

"Thank you. Plain is fine."

"I can take it back and put some syrup in it."

"Please, plain is fine."

"Well—I squeezed a lemon in it."

"Lemon is wonderful," I say. I take a sip.

"A child was killed?"

"Ismi! For fuck's sake! I'm talking to the police here."

Mr. Brewster's pupils are dilated. His sclera are red and full of veins. His shirt is askew by two buttons.

"But . . . a child . . ."

"Ismi."

"Thank you for the water, Mrs. Brewster—"

"Esmeralda, please."

"Of course, Esmeralda. It's very important that I ask your husband some questions now."

"Yes, yes. I understand. Coffee is in the French press. I'll leave you two alone for now."

"I appreciate it," I say.

"Arnold," I say once she's gone, "anything you can tell me about Beckett Shaw would be very helpful. Please. The people he's been spending time with. Any activities he's been up too. There are a lot of reports that he was live streaming on Instagram this morning, that he may have said some inflammatory things, but the video's been deleted, or he didn't save it publicly. And nobody seems to be able to confirm what he actually said, only that they're angry about it. Maybe you know his phone password? His recent associates?"

"I don't know his password. Why would I know his password?"

"Of course. I didn't expect you did. Was Beckett Shaw recently involved in any disputes? Did he upset anyone?"

"Not that I know of. Do you mind if I smoke?"

"It's your house," I say.

He reaches over the arm of the couch and retrieves a sea-green marble marijuana pipe.

"Had Beckett Shaw mentioned anything to you recently that might indicate why someone would want to kill him? Why someone would wish him harm?"

"Has he . . .?" Mr. Brewster fills the bowl of the pipe with dried marijuana leaves. I didn't see where he pulled the leaves from. He moves a couple couch cushions around. "Have you seen my lighter?"

"I'm afraid not. Mr. Brewster—"

"Arnold."

"Arnold, please, this is all very im—"

"Found it!" He lights the pipe and inhales. He coughs. He takes a deep breath.

"Arnold, it's very important that you tell me anything you can think of that Beckett Shawn might have said to you—"

"Fuck. I'm sorry." Mr. Brewster is coughing like a steam engine in an old cartoon. He coughs for a good thirty seconds. "Fuck me," he finally says, and then he takes another hit of his pipe.

"Arnold! Are you okay?" Mrs. Brewster yells from the other room.

"I'm fine, Ismi!"

"You sure?!"

"I said I'm fine!"

"Well okay then!"

"Sorry about that, Detective."

"It's all right. But now can you *please* tell me something about Beckett Shaw. Can you just *think*? Is there *something*?"

"I—"

"Yes?"

He's silent. He seems to be staring past me. I turn around. There's nothing but another abstract modernist painting. "Arnold?"

"I was just thinking that maybe it was the Republicans."

"I'm sorry?"

"The Republicans didn't like Beckett. Said he had loose morals."

"Which Republicans?"

"All—all of them." Mr. Brewster's eyes are glassy. He lets out a truncated cough.

"I don't understand."

"What?"

"You think the . . . Republicans killed Mr. Shaw. All of them."

Mr. Brewster shrugs. "What do I know?"

"Here we go," says Mrs. Brewster, returning and placing a mug of coffee on the coffee table in front of her husband.

"Do you take cream?" she says to me as places a second mug on the table.

"Oh—I don't need any—"

"I have almond milk, too. And soy. This here is soy"—she sets a small carafe on the table—"Arnold isn't allowed to have diary."

"I—"

"We might have oat milk, too, if you want. I can go check."

I've had oat milk. It tastes like shoes. "No, thank you, Esmeralda. Black is wonderful. Listen—Mrs. Brewster—has your husband taken anything?"

She looks mildly concerned. "Like what? Like *stolen* something?"

"No no no. Has he done any drugs—besides marijuana?"

"Oh, dear. I don't *think* so. Have you done any drugs, Arnold?"

"Jus' my statins," he says.

"Arnold has high blood pressure. But his doctor is working with him on it."

"Is not th' high."

"It's a little high, dear."

"You know—he was fucking Kennedy?"

"Who was what?" Mrs. Brewster says.

"Wait—Kennedy Thorne?"

"Yeppers. She was fuckin' him last night. What she told me."

"Oh my. Detective, I'm so sorry for Arnold's . . . inappropriate—"

"No no, it's fine. It might be helpful. Mr. Brewster, we knew Ms. Thorne and Mr. Shaw were associates. We suspected they might have had a romantic relationship, but last night? You're sure?"

"What she told me."

"You've spoke to Kennedy Thorne? Today?"

"Yeppers." He smiles.

"Mr. Brewster, do you know how I can get ahold of Kennedy Thorne?"

"Arnold," Mrs. Brewster says. "Can you help the detective?"

"Mr. Brewster?" I say. "Arnold? Mr. Brewster?"

"Oh dear," Mrs. Brewster says.

ADELINE

I attempt CPR while Mrs. Brewster calls an ambulance from the kitchen. I lay Arnold on his back on the couch and compress his chest with my hands, my right hand over my left, counting as I pump—but nothing happens. Mrs. Brewster reenters the room, a cordless phone to her ear. She looks at me pleadingly and I shrug. I hover my hand above his nostrils. "I think he's actually breathing," I tell her. "Tell them he's catatonic."

"He's catastrophic," Mrs. Brewster says.

"Cata*tonic*."

"Catatonic." She looks at me. "They're on their way. Oh dear—I do hope everything's okay. Yes—" she says into the phone. "I can stay on the line. I'm well—how are you?"

I pull out my phone to call this in, but I'm honestly entirely unsure what's going on, so I put it back. I try chest compressions again—gentle ones—but nothing happens. Arnold Brewster is definitely breathing. Each breath is shallow, ragged, and when I lean closer I realize he's wheezing, but I think it's because he's overweight, not because something particularly sinister is blocking his airway.

I take a sip of the coffee Mrs. Brewster prepared—but just one sip. I wait a moment and then there it is: the caffeine. I can feel it in my fingertips. The one sip is all I needed and all I wanted. It's tasty coffee—nutty, fruity, a hint of cherry and tobacco on my tongue.

The Brewsters' doorbell rings. "That was fast."

"That was fast," Mrs. Brewster repeats to the dispatcher. She listens. "Huh." She looks at me. "She says there's no way they're here yet."

I head into the foyer, my hand moving to my duty weapon. I peak through the peephole. *Ugh.* I open the door.

Paul is only one person, but somehow he comes pouring into the foyer, a flood of a man. "Did you *hear that?* Was that N.W.A? In a doorbell? That's fucking awesome. Fucking awesome."

"Paul—" I say.

"How's the interrogation going?"

"I'm not *interrogating* anyone."

"Right—of course. We don't interrogate. We 'interview.' What did the suspect have to say for himself?"

"Susp . . . ? Fuck, Paul, he's not a suspect. He's—"

"I know. I know. I'm joking. I think I have a real suspect for us, anyway. Or multiple suspects. It's fucking crazy. You're not going to believe— Damn, look at this place. What even is that supposed to be? A battlefield? Did someone jizz a rainbow across a battlefield?"

"It's art. Contemporary art."

"Sure it is. And I'm a goddamn double-oh agent."

"Paul—we have a situation here. Mr. Brewster is unresponsive."

"Oh? You want I should rough him up? Good cop bad cop?"

"No—what? No—I mean he's medically unresponsive."

"Oh. Oh shit."

"An ambulance is on the way."

"Where is he? I can help. I'm CPR certified."

"Of course you are. You're a cop." A fucking terrible cop. "I already tried. Like I said, he's *unresponsive*. His wife is on the phone with emergency dispatch."

Reluctantly, I lead Paul into the sitting room where Arnold Brewster still lies; I don't want Paul to contaminate the scene— or do anything else stupid. Mrs. Brewster looks at me imploringly. She covers the phone's mouthpiece. "They say they're just minutes away."

"Damn," Paul says. "That's a fat fucker. No wonder he's not breathing."

"Paul!" I grab his arm and pull him into the kitchen. "First, he *is* breathing. He's not dead. He's *unresponsive*. Second—" Fuck—what does one say to Paul? What does one ever say to Paul?

"I have news," Paul says. "About Beckett Shaw."

"What kind of news?" I glance around the kitchen. It's one of those big ones you might see in a home listing and think, I could never afford a kitchen like that. There's a dining table where Paul and I are standing. It's rectangular and art deco and has six chairs. There's a laptop on it—closed—and a short stack of newspapers, *LA Times* and *New York Times*. An empty water glass. This must be the breakfast table. I know this because there is a separate dining room off this room, through an archway, and I can see part of a sturdier wooden table with sturdier chairs, probably more than six of them, probably unused for some time. The kitchen itself, part of the same open space as the space that houses the breakfast table, also has a breakfast bar, and an island with a sink and a granite countertop—and there's a second sink inset in one of the counters, and two ovens—convection and whatever a regular oven is called?—and large refrigerator and a wine fridge with at least a dozen bottles of white wine. And on the countertops are a toaster and some sort of complicated coffee contraption that's obviously just been used and a SodaStream—but no food of any kind. I've become distracted. I've stopped hearing Paul. I focus first on my breath—just one—and then back on Paul, and that's when I realize he's saying something about Republicans. "What?" I say. "Say that again."

"I said it looks like Shaw may been involved in some sort of conspiracy. Something to do with the flat-earthers or the Republicans. Are they mutually exclusive? All Republicans aren't flat-earthers, right? Are all flat—"

Flat-earthers? I'm disappointed in myself for not paying attention to what Paul was saying—but self-shame will get me nowhere. "Quiet," I say. I half close my eyes and rewind back to when I first pulled Paul in here, moments ago. I have news, he said. And then . . . ? And then he said a guy called in and said Beckett Shaw had been posting on conspiracy forums in 8kun. Said the guy was sure it was Shaw even though he used a pseudonym in the forum. Said the guy said it was an open secret that Shaw had been sliding to the alt-right over the last year, although he didn't talk about it in his YouTube videos. I'm caught up. "Okay," I tell Paul. "Go on."

Paul shrugs. "That's pretty much it, really. The guy said Shaw was ranting about that sort of shit in his livestream this morning."

"'The guy?' Did you get a name?"

"He wished to remain anonymous."

"Does he have a recording of the livestream?"

Paul shakes his head. "No dice."

"This sounds implausible," I say.

"I agree, except it sounds like it could be true, right?"

"That's the opposite of implausible, but I don't know. Did you pull up records for the caller?"

Paul shrugs. "Tried to. Nothing available."

"Everything you said sounds like nonsense," I say, "except that before he went all catatonic, Arnold Brewster said something about Republicans too."

"Whoa. What about flat-earth people?"

"No—I think we can safely discount them."

"But you think it might be the Republicans?"

I look at him. "There's no such thing as 'The Republicans,' Paul."

"Now that can't be—"

"Shut up, I'm thinking."

But I can't think, because my attempts are interrupted by the sound of ambulance sirens. "That's the paramedics. I'll get the door. You go join Mrs. Brewster."

I don't know that having Paul in the same room as Mrs. Brewster is a good idea. But I don't know that having him greet the paramedics is either.

I open the front door. "The patient is this way."

"My god," one of the paramedics says after shining a light into Arnold Brewster's left eye. "What did he take?"

Mrs. Brewster says, "Just . . . Just his blood pressure medication."

"He smoked some marijuana," I say, pointing to the pipe on the floor.

"We'll take that," the other EMT says. "Maybe it was laced with something."

"Oh dear oh dear," says Mrs. Brewster.

Once the ambulance has driven away, Paul turns to Mrs. Brewster on the sidewalk and says, "Ma'am, we're going to need to ask you some more questions. Please don't go anywhere."

"But—but—"

"Paul, it's fine." To Mrs. Brewster I say, "It's fine. Go to the hospital with your husband."

Once she's returned to the house, Paul says, "But what about the investigation?"

"She doesn't know anything." Although I do think maybe she poisoned her husband—but that's an investigation I'm not interested in starting right now. "I need you to return to the precinct. Keep trying to track down that livestream. Put out a call for it on the department Twitter and a Facebook accounts. Somebody has to have screen-recorded it or something. And let's get a subpoena out to Facebook, even thought it'll probably take days for them to cooperate. And tell forensics to hurry up with whatever they have from the coffee shop."

"What about you?"

"I need to find Kennedy Thorne." I don't know why, but I need to find Kennedy Thorne. I pull out my cell phone to call her again. She doesn't answer.

KEELY

J-Sean is on the phone with a former client, telling them that, no, he can't refund a blazer he designed two years ago because a seam tore yesterday. He's saying, "I don't give a fuck if your fucking *mother* tripped and fell and broke her neck on the thread—I'm not refunding the fucking blazer."

I don't know who the client is—J-Sean has designed dozens of blazers—but they sound old. Which probably limits who they are to a small handful of people, but I'd have to stop and think about it to figure out who it might be, and I really don't want to do that right now.

J-Sean and I are upstairs in his loft. He's pacing. He has a cigarillo in one hand and his phone to his ear in the other. He looks at me, rolls his eyes. "Yes, if you bring it in *of course* I'll fix it. One hundred bucks. No, not today. Today is not a good day. Yes? That makes sense. I was wondering how the hell you could have possibly had time today, either."

I'm on J-Sean's bed, fielding incoming messages on my own phone. It's a wonder I haven't decided to get stoned yet today. I don't know what I'm going to do when all this is over.

I tweet, *Still thinking about fucking killing myself, although I'm sure I won't. Don't @ me.*

I told Leilani not to destroy the dress. Told her don't even touch it. It's kind of already destroyed, she said, so I told her if she destroyed the dress further I would fire her. I'm not sure I can fire her, but I can convince J-Sean to. If I can convince him not to fire Renalda, I can convince him to fire Leilani. I told Leilani that she and Maurice had two hours to fix the dress.

"What about my finger?" Maurice said.

"You better put it on ice."

I get a text from Leilani now: *Making progress. It's vaguely pinkish. Only vaguely.*

I want it white. We need it white.

Working on it.

"No, not tomorrow. I'm doing fuck all tomorrow, darling, and I imagine so are you. Yes, Tuesday, then. Tuesday is fine," J-Sean says. "You shouldn't wear something you already own to the Oscars anyway. Everyone will know."

Interesting. I think I was wrong about the client being an old person. Everyone will know or care if they're not wearing new clothes on the red carpet only if they're a woman—nobody pays attention to that sort of thing for men. So, let's see: J-Sean designed a blazer for a woman . . . who wants to wear it to the Oscars. . . . Could it really be Lady Gaga on the phone? I mean, I guess. . . . Who else would have J-Sean's cell phone number?

"You, too, Stef," J-Sean says. "Love you too. Byeee." He throws the phone on the bed. "Tough day, man," he says.

"Word," I say.

"You hear from that Kennedy Thorne bitch yet?"

"Can't get ahold of her."

"Fucking selfish bitch. You untag her?"

"Yes."

"Good. Don't delete the photo, though. Not yet. Just keep her untagged. Imma go take a shit."

I call Kennedy Thorne for the fourth time. No answer. Leilani sends me a photo from downstairs. *Too pink*, I type back.

What if we soak the whole thing? she says.

Could you get it dry in time?

Probably not.

Then no.

Fuck.

You'll figure it out.

Fuck you.

I sigh. I do not sigh often. I would like to go see a movie. I would like to go to The Matinee tonight and do some cocaine. It's Sunday. I should not even be here on a Sunday. J-Sean doesn't like to work on Sundays, and neither do I. Fuck the Oscars. Fuck Hollywood. Says the girl who lives in Hollywood, the girl who moved to Hollywood so she could work with Hollywood.

J-Sean's phone buzzes briefly near my feet. I glance at it but I don't move for it. Sometimes I answer his personal phone for him, but only if he tells me to. The phone buzzes again. Then it stops. J-Sean, I realize, doesn't have his phone with him in the bathroom. How the fuck is he shitting without his phone to look at? I know that's how people used to do it, but I can't fathom how anyone could do it these days. Maybe he looks at fashion magazines. I've never been in his personal bathroom.

I check my own personal email. I check my own personal Twitter. Nobody has responded to my suicide tweet. Three people have favorited it. I have 937 followers because J-Sean retweets me sometimes. Or I retweet myself from his account and he doesn't mind.

J-Sean comes out of the bathroom.

"You got a text, I think," I tell him.

He picks up his phone, unlocks it by looking at it. "Awww. It's Stephanie again."

"Lady Gaga Stephanie?"

"Yeah. She has extra invites to the after party at Ménage à Trois tonight. I fuckin' love that bitch. You wanna go with me?"

"Me?"

"Yeah, you."

"What about Stuart?"

"He'll be too high to enjoy it by then. Besides, you shouldn't even be working on a Sunday. Let's take tomorrow off, go get fucked up tonight. Tuesday we'll talk about giving you a raise."

I sit up. "Really? A raise?"

"Sure, why not? You're a great assistant."

"Thanks, J-Sean."

"It's whatever."

"Fuck—thanks. I really appreciate it."

"It's whatever. Hey—I'm feeling pretty chill. Damn—that Thorne bitch's dress is a good dress. You think Leilani actually burned it yet?"

"Not exactly," I say.

He's quite for a moment. He finally says, "Fuck . . . She should probably wear it—"

J-Sean's phone begins to buzz. It's a sustained buzz. He looks at the screen. "Unidentified caller." He hands the phone to me. "You answer it."

"Hello?" I say. "J-Sean Laurentius's studio. Keely speaking."

"Yes, hello. This Detective Adeline Ramos. I'm investigating a homicide and I need to speak to Miss Kennedy Thorne—"

"Kennedy Thorne killed someone?!"

J-Sean says, "Say what?"

I put the phone on speaker.

"No, no," the detective (if she's really a detective) says. "But she knew the deceased and I need to ask her some questions. I haven't been able to get ahold of her on the phone. I understand she has an appointment with you today."

I look at J-Sean. "She was here earlier. I don't think she'll be back . . . ?"

J-Sean shrugs and then nods.

"I guess she *will* be back," I say. "At . . . two-thirty?"

"May we stop by?"

J-Sean shrugs.

"Sure," I say.

"Great. We'll see you then."

"Fuuuck," J-Sean says after I give the phone back to him. He draws out the word. Fuuuuck. He looks around. "Okay—well. Imma hide any drugs layin' around up here. You go check on the dress."

"So she's uncancelled?"

He shrugs again. "If she apologizes and posts that fuckin' photo. I wanna know if she killed someone."

"I don't think she—"

"Fuuuck"—he draws the word out again—"today just got interesting."

I sigh again, stand from the bed, and send Leilani another text as I follow J-Sean down the stairs.

KENNEDY

I don't think it was today that I lost myself, to be honest, although I'm not sure when it was.

I remember there was a time when I was a little girl who liked to play softball and watch *Seinfeld* reruns with her father even though she didn't get the jokes. My father has had gray hair as long I can remember. "Salt and pepper" is what he used to call it when I was very young—when my mother would touch his hair and make a comment about how gray it was. He would correct her: "Salt and pepper." As if to make it clear that it wasn't all gray, that the jet-blackness of his youth still existed up there, somewhere. As I got older, his hair stayed the same, but he started, too, to refer to it as gray.

I haven't talked to my father in four or five weeks. How long ago was Christmas? Whenever Christmas was, that's when I last called my father. And my mother. Christmas was when I last called her, too. Christmas Eve. I wonder what they're doing right now? Watching *The Office* on Netflix? At Christmas when I called them my father said, "Did you know *Seinfeld* is on Hulu now? They have all the episodes!"

"He's watched three seasons so far this week," my mother said.

"What else am I gonna do?" my father said. He finally retired late last year, after five years in the military and 39 as a mailman.

"We wish you could have made it back this year," my mom said. "Nanna's been asking about you."

How is Nanna not dead yet? How does Nanna even remember my name?

"We got your DVD. We're gonna watch your movie tomorrow, the whole family, after we open presents."

When I was four years old my father bought me a tee-ball set and took me out to the back yard to play with it. I think this is my first memory. His hair was gray even then. He has a beard in this memory. The beard is gray, too. It's short but not stubby. His hair is gray gray gray, but it might be accurate to call the beard salt and pepper. We're in the backyard, by the big tree. My father has set the tee up so that, in relation to where I stand to hit the ball, the big tree is just a few feet behind me and to the left. We're facing the house. The house is some distance away. I'm only four and know neither imperial nor metric measurements.

My father balances the ball atop the tee and then places the bat into my hands. He shows me how to hold the bat. The bat, the ball—the whole tee-ball set—all of it is made of plastic. The tee is red and sturdy, the bat is yellow and hollow, the ball is white with holes in it, the size of a regular baseball or maybe just slightly larger, and the bat is the size and shape of a regulation baseball bat, just plastic and hollow.

"This is how you hold the bat," my father says. He has me step away from the tee and suggests I take a couple swings into the air—to get a feel for things. I swing. I swing. I swing. I am a Jedi, is the first thing I think of, because I have more experience with Star Wars at four years old than I do with sports.

"Nice job," my father says. "Now come back over here and try to hit the ball."

I set myself up behind and to the left of the tee. So if you were to look down on our yard from above you would see the big tree, my father, me, the tee, all points on an invisible diagonal line. If I hit the ball, the trajectory of the ball connected to the line on which we are points would make an obtuse angle. My teacher will tell me a few years later that you can remember obtuse versus acute because obtuse sounds like obese and acute sounds like cute and little. I will realize a decade after that how very cruel this heuristic is. In any case, I don't hit the ball. I try to hit it, but I swing high.

"That's okay," my father says. "Now you know that you swing high, so you can adjust for that. You just need to adjust a little, a little downward."

Again, I swing high.

"That's quite all right," he says. "Here, see, just keep your eye on the ball. Don't think about the bat. Just look right there at the ball and then swing your arms. Follow through with your swing. Don't forget to follow through."

We spend all afternoon in the yard by the big tree. I cannot hit the ball.

Sometimes as I was growing up my father had that beard and sometimes he did not. The beard was not a constant like the grayness of his hair. This isn't a matter of chronology. He just couldn't seem to make up his mind about the beard.

"I like it," my mother would say.

"I just don't know . . ." would reply my father. And a few days later the beard would be gone, only to begin to grow again.

"The new back deck is nearly finished," my mother told me when we spoke on the phone at Christmas.

"The contractors sure took their sweet time with it," my father said.

"You heard them," said my mother. "They had to make sure it was regulation."

"Regulation my ass," said my father. "We shouldn't have agreed to pay them by the day. We should have negotiated a lump sum for the whole damn project."

"Well, in any case, it's nearly done. They weren't able to work on it last week because the snow, and of course now it's the holiday, but as soon as New Year's is over they say they'll be right back to work and have it done in just a few more days."

"I don't know why we had a deck built in the winter."

"I just didn't want to wait."

"Would have been cheaper if we'd waited."

"Yes, well. It's almost done. And it looks great, Kennedy. Wait until you get to see it. I'll make you some iced tea and we'll sit out there and talk about all the things."

Beckett never spoke to me about his father or his mother. He mentioned a brother once—a brother who he said had "severely disappointed the family." He didn't say any more than that about his brother. So when Arnold told me Beckett was a rich kid with a trust fund, I was surprised. I shouldn't have been surprised—I always knew Beckett had money. His flat, though smaller than mine, was even nicer. He spent like he had money. His flat had a heated floor in the bathroom, and the shower glass was not just frosted but etched. And, although we did not go out often, Beckett and I, when we went out he insisted on paying every time. He surprised me with those Comedy Store tickets. We went out for dinner once, he ordered steak, I ordered fish, and at the end he surprised me with a creme brûlée, still on fire. Beckett liked to surprise me.

But it's true what Arnold said: Beckett didn't work much. I'm not even a YouTuber and yet at my own flat I have a decently expensive camera and an iMac that Arnold insisted I purchase, and I use them to record and edit videos from time to time and post them on my Instagram. Unboxing videos, morning thoughts (after I've put on just enough makeup that it doesn't look like I've put on any makeup), that sort of thing. Because the secret about becoming an influencer I was told when I first started posting was that the best influencers use expensive cameras and editing software as much as they use their phone. But Beckett . . . he had a channel with nearly a million followers and he *only* used his phone . . . in handheld mode . . . no tripod even. But I never saw him recording or editing or posting. Don't you need to work? I asked him one morning after he suggested we spend the day together.

"Nah," he said. "I make a point of not having a schedule. I make a point of spending each day as I want to, of living life as my heart compels me."

I asked him doesn't that get boring? Doesn't that get exhausting, not knowing what you're going to do next?

"Not for me. It's the most vital part of freedom. Letting no one control your life, your actions, your *thoughts*."

Your thoughts?

"Oh yes. If you just stop for a minute and watch your thoughts, you'll realize they're not yours. They've been put there by someone else, nearly all of them. By your parents, by your culture, by your religious leaders."

I told him I don't have any religious leaders.

"Neither do I. But the thoughts are there. The thoughts have been there for millenia."

I asked him what about Arnold? Arnold was Beckett's agent, too.

Beckett laughed. "Well, I haven't achieved total freedom yet. Arnold is a persuasive guy. But today I have nothing to do."

Well, I told him, my calendar was full today. A full calendar, to me, I told him, felt like freedom, and money, and like people knowing my name.

In another memory of my father I'm eleven years old and he doesn't have the beard and he's coaching my girls softball team. I've learned to swing the bat by now. I've learned to hit the ball. I've also learned to throw the ball in such a way that it's very hard to hit. I should be the pitcher, and I usually am, but today at practice I'm playing right field so that another girl can practice pitching, and I'm bored. No one ever hits the ball out here. But someone *does* hit the ball out here this time, and it's coming at me, and I can't see it because the sun is in my eyes. "Kennedy, watch out!" my father yells. I raise my glove, both to catch the ball and block out the sun, but I'm off by a couple inches. "Kennedy!"

In the emergency room my father is told I have a concussion, but it's a small one, and they'd like to keep an eye on me for an hour or two. My father is beside himself with guilt. My mother is on her way. I tell my father it's okay, I feel completely normal, my forehead is just a little tender is all. This is the first and only time I see my father cry.

"So what's George Clooney like?" my mother asked when we spoke on the phone at Christmas.

GWEN

This is DINO. DINO is a peer-to-peer distributed social network built upon a node.js framework. To use DINO, send a message to @Ev using Scuttlebutt. @Ev will forward your request over a secure, encrypted connection to @Gwen, who will send you an invite via email (please provide your email address when messaging @Ev via Scuttlebutt) with a link to set up your own DINO distro. @Ev will respond to your initial Scuttlebutt message with your own personal DINO decryption key. Please keep this key handy. You will need it whenever you log on to DINO. In the event you lose your DINO decryption key, we will not be able to generate a new one. Your DINO @ name will be lost and you will have to restart the process.

Note: to do the above, you will need a device with command line access. No iPhones here.

@Gwen @Ev is off to work and probably won't be back until late tonight (he doesn't close but he'll still probably be one of the last people let go from his shift), so I'm at the apartment by myself working on some new updates to DINO and diving into this Beckett Shaw thing. I'm not sure what to make of it. CNN says it was a robbery gone wrong, but the

New York Times is reporting that it's being investigated as a deliberate homicide. Rachel Maddow is speculating a connection to the Russians for some reason. LAPD is asking—begging—anyone who has one to come forward with a recording of a livestream Shaw did on Instagram. Surely Instagram has a recording. Is there anyone out there on DINO who knows how to go about hacking in and getting that?

@Gwen Anyone?

@Gwen Anyone?

@Gwen I've made a few updates to my DINO distro. Message replies should come through much faster now. @ me if you want the code so you can modify your own distro, or find it on Git. Gonna go do a couple Namaskaras, eat a hoagie, and make a fourth cup of coffee. I'll reply to anyone who messages me when I get back.

@Gwen Howdy @VV3kSt0rk. Welcome to DINO. Let me know if you have any questions.

@Gwen Interesting . . . May have a lead on the Beckett Shaw video . . .

KEELY

J-Sean is by the wet bar drinking an espresso with caffeine that Renalda made him from the espresso maker and eating a pepperoni stick with his bare hands. J-Sean doesn't do caffeine in the morning because he says it makes him jittery and interferes with his creativity, but in the afternoon he drinks it because he "needs a pick-me-up" and doesn't know how else he "could possibly focus when everyone's talking to me at all those parties." As for the pepperoni stick:

"I know I'm vegan and all but you also gotta eat the meat from time to time," he explains to the detective. "Gotta get that protein and that B12. We evolved to eat meat, you know. Hundred million years we ate meat, so even us vegans gotta eat it some times. Sad about the animals though."

The detective holds a glass of sparkling water. She said "we" on the phone but she showed up all by herself.

Kennedy Thorne isn't here. Kennedy Thorne is running late. I assume Kennedy Thorne is running late but I still haven't been able to get ahold of her, so I'm not sure.

J-Sean is talking to the detective about meditation. I've never seen him meditate. But—apparently—it's something he's been doing every morning for years, he's telling her.

I slip into the workshop where the lights are still dim. "How's it coming?"

"I can't feel my hand," Maurice says.

"We're just about done," says Leilani. "We had some more of this silk in storage and I was able to take J-Sean's original pattern and replicate this section here. I'm just finishing up the stitching." She moves the dress deftly beneath a sewing machine.

"You think it will hold?"

"It's a bit of a rush job given the circumstances, but the Oscars only last like, what, three hours? And they change clothes before the after parties, right? Nothing's gonna fall apart by then."

"I don't think they're going to be able to put my fingertip back on," says Maurice.

"We're lucky the Thorne girl hasn't shown up yet," Leilani says. "It took me forever to find the extra fabric, and for some reason there was no more off-white thread, like, anywhere."

"What about this part?" I ask.

"It's still a little pink, isn't it? But I can't replace that section. The lacing will take forever. But it's tight enough that I think it'll just look like shadows from the patterning. What do you think?"

I'm skeptical. "I won't be able to tell for sure until we get it under some real lights. It might be okay."

"The part that's still attached to my hand is turning black," Maurice says. "Under the bandage. I checked."

"How much longer?" I ask.

"How long do I have?"

I check my watch. "I don't know. Still no messages or calls. But for all I know she could be right outside."

"So even if they *can* reattach the tip they're going to have to cut off the black part. So my finger is going to be shorter."

"Almost done," Leilani says.

KENNEDY

Another memory I have is of my college boyfriend Ricky saying "Holy shit! Babe! Have you checked your Instagram lately?" We're upstairs in my bedroom at my parents' house. I think Ricky's high. His eyes are red. I've asked him whether he smokes weed or does drugs and he says he doesn't, but I know he's lying. Soon he'll convince me to try weed and I'll do it and be stoned for a long time before I quit and decide never to smoke it again. "Babe! You got six hundred and fifty-two likes on that photo of you in the yellow bathing suit. You're nearly at three thousand followers. Here, I have an idea. Take your shirt off. Imma take a photo, but, like a tasteful one, from behind. I'll write the caption. It's gonna be beautiful. Super inspiring and shit."

It got some likes, the photo of my back, before I started doing yoga and Peloton, when my back was nothing special but still feminine and not too broad or muscular, but I wouldn't become one of those IG models who posts only half-naked photos. I'd start first as a "comedian," telling Ricky's jokes, starring in his single-woman sketches. Until he realized it was me everyone was watching. Nobody cared about his writing.

Ricky couldn't act. Ricky didn't have the face for social media. I tagged him in every post of mine but his follower count hardly ever budged. "Someday soon Seth Rogan will see one of these and ask me to collaborate," he said. "Or Jimmy Fallon's gonna see it and have me on his show. Or even Lorne Michaels, and I'll write for SNL." But none of that happened. Ricky just smoked weed and kept living at his mother's house. And I smoked weed with him at his mother's house. And went to community college in the daytime. Until brands started sending me stuff. Only sometimes would I post half-naked photos. Like once every few months. Always with something inspiring or motivational below it. I don't know what Ricky did. Maybe he moved to New York. I like to think he moved to New York and does stand-up comedy.

"I was looking at your profile," said Beckett one evening after we'd fucked. He was lighting a joint. He offered me a hit and I said no. He took one hit himself and then set it down. ("This'll just help me sleep.") "Anyway, I was looking at your profile and you used to do all sorts of funny stuff. What happened to all that?"

I shrugged. "I think I just grew up. I think it was just time to get more serious."

"No, I don't think that's it. You're plenty serious in those clips. They're funny, but it's not *you* being funny. You're being serious about being funny, about presenting the material—I can tell. Being out there means a lot to you."

"Lots of things mean a lot to me. Everything means a lot to me."

Beckett looked at me. He seemed to examine me for a long time. "No," he finally said, "I don't think that's true."

The first couple times I fucked Beckett I didn't sleep over, but then suddenly I did. He didn't ask me to—it just happened. I fell asleep with his cum on my tits and on my neck and face and in my hair. After that I always slept over, or he slept over at my flat. We fucked at either my flat or his flat and every time either he slept over or I did. Once or twice a week or more. Then one day he said let's get dinner first. And he bought me tickets to the Comedy Store. And dinner became a regular thing. Dinner and talking and sex and talking and sleep and in the morning talking, sometimes sex again. But we were just fucking. He was the only guy I was fucking there for a while, but I don't think I was the only woman he was. But still—we were just fucking. Isn't that what I told Arnold? Beckett was just a body to hold on to at night.

But he's a body I'll never be able to hold on to again, is what the headlines and posts all said—and I just don't know that I can believe that yet.

ADELINE

As a detective in Los Angeles, it's not unusual for me to engage with celebrities. It would be *more* common if I were a beat cop—domestic disputes amongst the Hollywood elite are a near-nightly occurrence for the LAPD—but it's not at all *un*common. I once had to investigate, for example, an accidental stuntman death on the set of a Michael Bay movie, during which investigation I spoke to Mark Wallberg, Jane Fonda, and Michael Bay himself.

Last week I saw Daniel Craig in a coffee shop. I was with Paul. He freaked out. It was objectively embarrassing. Embarrassment is an unpleasant feeling.

More than one celebrity attends the weekly meditation group I've been struggling to get to regularly since Eva died. I will not disclose who they are out of respect for their spiritual privacy and personal safety.

Suffice it to say, many of the stars with whom I've interacted have had their eccentricities. But that's because all people have their eccentricities, and celebrities are people. I get that. I'm neither star-struck nor resentful whenever these interactions occur. I am occasionally amused by, say, the inability of an actress famous for her monologues to look you in the eye or speak at a volume louder than a mumble during day-to-day conversation, or by a popular Fortnite streamer's terrible breath, or by a well-known action star's refusal to take a flight of stairs lest he trip and hurt himself—but they're all still people.

J-Sean Laurentius, however, gives the impression of being something else. As he proudly shows me a design he's been working for months on, I pick up from him an energy I've never quite experienced anywhere else.

"I been wantin' for a long time to get into the jewelry game," he's saying, "but it's, like, haaaard, man. Ma'am. Yo, can I ask your pronouns?"

"She/her," I say.

"Cool, that's cool. That's what I thought, but, you know, don't want to assume. Can I call you 'hon'?"

"Um . . . sure."

"I didn't want to assume. So I was sayin', this is called a Celtic knot, and it's really tough to design one that looks good, in my opinion. I've been working on a few different materials, but I just can't seem to find one I like, right? Gold, silver, brass —everybody's done them before, and it's like, whatever, you know? Plus the knot is just a knot. There's nothing *special* about it. It's this cool, weird design that looks all complicated and shit, but it's really just like, whatever. But *then*"—he turns a page in his sketchbook—"I was like, wait a second—what if I made a necklace that's *a bunch* of Celtic knots made from Celtic knots? And I was like, holy shit!"

The sketch is impressive, I'm compelled to admit. I scan the room, hoping Kennedy Thorne is walking through the entrance, but she is not. She is at least 30 minutes late. "That is very . . . cool," I tell J-Sean Laurentius.

"I know, right? But still, I'm not sure about the material. I been 3D-printing a few different variations of the design and spraypainting them and handpainting them and even doing this air-blasting thing, all sorts of different colors, and it's like, nah. I did one in actual silver—cost me a fuckton—but it was like, I can't let anyone wear this. So, yeah, I dunno, you know, hon?"

"Sure," I reply. "That sounds tough."

He tilts his head to the side and his expression softens. "It *is*. Thank you so much for saying that."

"Do you have an update on Miss Thorne, by any chance?"

"Let me check. KEELY!"

The assistant with whom I spoke on the phone and who greeted me when I first arrived appears from somewhere. "Nothing, J-Sean," she says. "I've been calling her and texting her, but there's only so much I can do. I called her agent, but he didn't pick up, either."

"Oh—" I say. "Don't bother with her agent. I've already spoken to him." I don't disclose his current situation because that feels unethical. "He . . . doesn't know where she is."

"Well shit," says J-Sean. "Am I right?"

"You sure I can't get you something to drink, Detecive?" Keely asks.

"Thank you," I say. "I suppose I will have some water."

"We got sparkling," says J-Sean. "We got a SodaStream. We got Topo Chico. We got flavored. We got CBD-infused. We got filtered. We got—"

"Regular will be fine, thanks. Excuse me—I'm going to make a quick call."

I step to a relatively quiet corner of the studio and pull out my phone. "Paul," I say after he answers.

"What's up?"

"You tell me. Anything new?"

"Sorry, partner. Nothing."

"Damn."

"No, wait, sorry. Forensics came back on the third bullet. The one we found behind the pastry case."

Before I can stop them, my eyes roll. "That's *something*, Paul. What did they find?"

"The bullet came from a barrel with a left-handed twist."

That means a Colt. Only weapons manufactured by Colt have left-handed twists. But how does this help us? I present this question to Paul.

"Oh, yeah, that's the other thing—we got a call about a body found in a dumpster behind an abandoned shopping center in El Segundo."

"Okay?"

"The body was fresh. Super fresh. Male. Mid-twenties. Hispanic. Some homeless guy found him. Well so I guess the precinct over there had, like, nothing going on today, because they got a forensics team on the scene fast. Get this—this guy has powder on his jeans. *Gun*powder. On the waist of his pants, like he keeps a gun tucked into his pants like an idiot. So a guy I know at the South Bureau station shoots me a text to tell me about the idiot they found who keeps a gun in his pants, and I call him—kind of on a whim—and send him the forensics on our bullet and guess what—"

"The powder on his pants matched the residue at the scene."

"The powder on his pants— Wait—how'd you know?"

"Because this story is taking forever, Paul, and I know you wouldn't be telling me if it wasn't going to end one way. When did this happen?"

"Just found out ten minutes ago."

"How'd you get the results so fast?"

"My guy at South Bureau owed me a favor. I let him sleep on my couch for a month during his divorce last year."

"Of course you did. We need to get someone to where they found the body."

"I'm already on my way. You wanna meet me?"

I look around the studio. The assistant holds a glass of water in my direction. "You head there first," I say. "Text me the location. Thorne hasn't shown up yet, but I'm going to give her thirty more minutes. Then I'll meet you."

"Sounds like a plan."

It *is* a plan. I make the plans. Don't fuck it up, Paul, I think as I end the call.

A few seconds later Paul sends the address through. So far so good, then. Paul isn't the worst at taking instructions, as long as you give them with a clear, confident voice. He knows his job. He didn't become a full-blown detective by being completely atrocious at it.

I hold my phone in my hand and examine its straight, convex edges as a grounding exercise. I consider calling the daycare center so that I can hear Jessie's voice. But then J-Sean Laurentius comes over, and he's holding an object.

"Yo. So . . . I was just thinking, right? Apple's been making these watches out of titanium lately. *Titanium!*"

EV & GWEN & VV3KST0RK

This is DINO. DINO is a peer-to-peer distributed social network built upon a node.js framework. To use DINO, send a message to @Ev using Scuttlebutt. @Ev will forward your request over a secure, encrypted connection to @Gwen, who will send you an invite via email (please provide your email address when messaging @Ev via Scuttlebutt) with a link to set up your own DINO distro. @Ev will respond to your initial Scuttlebutt message with your own personal DINO decryption key. Please keep this key handy. You will need it whenever you log on to DINO. In the event you lose your DINO decryption key, we will not be able to generate a new one. Your DINO @ name will be lost and you will have to restart the process.

Note: to do the above, you will need a device with command line access. No iPhones here.

@Ev Hey, @Gwen. I'm on break. I just hopped over to the Starbucks next door so I could use their WiFi to check in on the Beckett Shaw situation. Bought a muffin and a double espresso. The espresso tastes like shit. I've got six minutes before I have to get back to the restaurant. What's the situation?

@Gwen @Ev! Meet @VV3kSt0rk. Dude sent me a link to a private server hosting a recording of the Shawn livestream from this morning.

@Ev @VV3kSt0rk, nice to meet you. Can you share?

@VV3kSt0rk @Ev You're at Starbucks?

@Ev @VV3kSt0rk Running through a VPN, of course.

@VV3kSt0rk @EV You got Tor?

@Ev @VV3kSt0rk Course. Also—working through the command line right now.

@VV3kSt0rk @Ev Kay. Here's the access link.

@Ev @VV3kSt0rk Damn. 19 minutes. I don't have time to watch that.

@Gwen @Ev the important stuff is just in the last two.

@Ev @Gwen @VV3kSt0rk Watched it. Huh. We thinking some kind of domestic terrorist attack?

@Gwen That's what I'm thinking.

@Ev @VV3kSt0rk How'd you get this? You work for Facebook?

@Gwen @Ev I think he just deleted his distro.

@Ev @Gwen Damn.

@Gwen @Ev what do you want to do with this?

@Ev @Gwen I got to get back to work . . . I have someone covering my tables, but my boss is gonna be pissed if I'm not back, like, now.

PAUL

I remember this place. I used to come here when I was a kid, with my mom, when they first built it. There was a Payless here. Was where I got my shoes. And a check-cashing place. They gave my mom a loan she never did get herself out from under. I think that's why she started drinking, why she started hitting me and my brother.

But now the place is dead, empty. A big picture window on one of the storefronts is boarded up. There are vehicles in the parking lot, though. A white van, a black van, and an off-white Ford Fusion with an Uber sticker in the window. I slow my car and take a picture of each of the license plates. I text them to Adeline and to Chuck at the station. *Run these*, I say.

I drive slowly around the back of the building. There's no one here. Fuck. My guy at South Bureau said there'd be someone here to meet me, but it looks like they've got the scene cleaned up. That was fast. I park, get out of my car. Walk over to the two dumpsters at the rear of the building.

I pull myself to the top of one of the dumpsters and look inside it. It's empty. I check the other one: a few garbage bags, black ones and white ones, and a smattering of building materials, plywood and drywall, but that's it. Smells awful. I imagine these dumpsters aren't emptied regularly since nobody's supposed to be here.

"I already told 'em I don't know nothing more than that I found the guy," says a voice behind me. There's a man, large beard, denim jacket and denim pants, both filthy, smells as bad as the dumpster.

"Hey there," I say, dropping down.

"I was jus'— I was jus' lookin' for some'n ta eat when I found him."

"Did you get something to eat? Did the other officers— did they hook you up with anything?"

He shakes his head quickly.

"Come on," I say. "I got a Snickers in my squad car."

As he eats the Snickers I ask him, "You . . . stay around here?"

He looks at me. He jerks his head back.

"In the building?"

He shakes his head vigorously. "Can't get in. 'S locked."

"Of course."

"But someone's in there."

"What?"

He takes another bite of the Snickers. "I hear them. At night. Ghosts. Hollering."

"Ghosts. The ghosts drive those vans out front?"

He shrugs. "Maybe."

"Here, have another candy bar." I toss the guy a Twix. I have a whole stash in my car.

I walk back to the front of the building. I try the door of one of the storefronts but it doesn't open. I try another and it does. I think this was the Payless. I enter through the door and I'm in this big, dark space, empty except for some broken metal shelves and fixtures strewn across the floor, with a door at the back. I try that door but it doesn't open, won't even budge.

I leave the derelict Payless and walk around to the side of the building. There's a door here, big and solid. I pull the handle and it surprises me by opening just fine, creaking metallically. There's a light on inside.

SOP is that if I'm going to enter a building like this I'm supposed to let Adeline know and call for additional backup, but I don't feel like waiting. I've never been one to follow SOP. People think I'm a bad cop, a bad detective, but I'm not. I just don't think there's much use in doing things the "right way." In taking the time to consider people's "feelings." In going through the "proper channels." That's not how you get shit done. Being a cop is about instinct. Listening to your fucking heart. And right now my heart is telling me there's something going on inside this building and everyone at South Bureau was too stupid to even look into it. But I'm not stupid. And I'm here. Backup isn't. Adeline isn't.

I let the door close behind me. I draw my service weapon. Why are the lights on?

CARLOS

"Someone's entered the building," says one of the guys who's name I don't remember. He's looking at his phone screen.

"Shit," says Anders.

"It's a cop," the guy says.

"Double shit. I thought they all left."

"They did," says Crowder.

Vickers says, "Fuck, Anders. I shouldn't have put Juan in the dumpster. That was amateur. That was something Juan himself would have done."

"Not your fault," Anders says. "Another hour and we would have been gone. Another three and it wouldn't have mattered whether they found the body. Our job would have been done."

"Fuck," says Vickers.

"It's okay. No reason to change the plan. Just a small obstacle to deal with before we get out of here." He looks at the guy who's monitoring his phone. "Just the one cop?"

"Yes."

"Check the outside cameras."

"Just the homeless guy. Empty cop car. Doesn't appear to be anybody else here. . . . Confirmed. The cop came alone."

"See," says Anders. "Just a small obstacle."

"I'll handle it," Crowder says.

"Take Carlos here with you."

"Take *him*?"

"I want him to understand how serious this all is."

"Ah—of course."

"Good. The rest of you, out the front, into the vans. We'll wait out the rest of the afternoon at Neutral Location A. This place is too hot. Crowder, Van 2 will wait for you."

"Got it."

"Good. Everyone, move out."

"Follow me," Crowder says. "And take this. It was Juan's. You ever shoot before?"

I stare at the cold gun he's just placed into my hand. I shake my head.

"It's easy. Point and squeeze. Follow through on the squeeze. No way you'll be worse than Juan was. Follow me," he says again.

I follow him into the hallway.

"By the way," he adds. "Don't you dare point it at me. Don't even try it. You'll never stand a chance."

PAUL

This place feels haunted. You've seen hallways like this one before, in movies: the walls are a sort of vomit-colored brick, green or gray or beige, it's hard to tell; wide enough for two average-size men to walk side by side, but no more; there are fluorescent light fixtures on the ceiling, running down the length of the place, but they're dimmer than fluorescent lights should be, ghostly, flickering too. But the floor is carpeted, which doesn't seem right. My steps don't echo as I walk. I want to call out, "Is anybody there?" but know that wouldn't be wise.

When do you ever do what's wise? I hear Adeline whisper in my ear. She's right, but still I don't call out. My service weapon is raised in front of me. I remind myself that I'm the one who's raised it. I am in charge here. I am a great detective.

"Hello?" I'm calling out. Damn it, Paul. Why did you do that? "LAPD! Come out with—" With what? "—with your hands up!"

Idiot.

I am walking down the corridor. Hallway. Corridor? I think corridors are on ships. Hallways are everywhere else. Maybe.

There's a door to my right. Holding my gun close with my right hand, I turn the knob with my left. No lights on in here. Should have brought a flashlight.

Looks like the room is empty. Moving on. Back to the haunted hallway.

I count three more doors—I swear they weren't there before—and then it looks like, maybe 20 yards from where I'm standing, the hallway converges with another hallway in a T shape.

Okay. Game plan. Check each of the three doors. One two three. Then, once I get to the end of the hallway, make a decision as to which direction to go.

The doors are staggered, alternating sides. Door one, on my left. I open it. Another dark room. Enough light leaks in that I can see two abandoned desks. A few scattered sheets of paper. One of the desks has a phone on it, with buttons.

I retreat. Back to the hallway.

I creep forward. Heel toe. Heel toe. Just like the Indian Americans.

Door on the right. Locked? No, just stuck. I switch my gun to my left hand and power into the door with my right shoulder. I am not left-handed, but occasionally I practice at the range with my left hand.

This room is large, like a small warehouse. It has its own fluorescent lights and I can see shelves and shelves, all empty. There are . . . beds? . . . along one wall? What the hell? These beds look slept in. I venture into the room. Definitely, bizarrely, slept in. Behind me—

I turn, gun high in both hands. Nothing there. No one there.

My phone buzzes in my pocket but I don't check it. I want to look under the beds, but I don't want to turn my back again. Back to the doorway. I peek left. I peek right. I re-enter the hallway and proceed via my previous route. One door left, on my left—but then I hear something echo from where this hallway meets the next hallways and it's unmistakably a real sound. I continue past the door, quickly, quickly. I like to think I'm fleet of foot and light as air, despite all the sandwiches and candy bars. I drink my vegetables every day.

Left or right? Left or right?

Left! Left! No one there, fewer fluorescent lights on the ceiling though. This hallway gets darker and darker and appears to go on impossibly long—surely longer than the building was outside. This hall's walls have wooden panels the other hallway didn't have. Behind me! I turn—

Something hits my kidney. Something hot. My intestines are far away and on fire.

CARLOS

The cop staggers forward but continues to turn around and the next thing I know, Crowder has put two bullets through the side of his head. Blood or brain matter splatters across the wall. The cop hits the floor, shoulder first, then face.

Everything is quiet, abandoned. I can feel my heart beating again. Surely I am going to die.

"Nice work!" Crowder says, placing a hand on my shoulder. "I didn't think you had it in you, honestly. Thought I was gonna have to shoot you and tell Anders you just didn't work out. But—fuck man—good shot. Better than Juan ever did, that's for sure. I mean, yeah, I had to finish him off, and he might have got us if I didn't, but for your first time handling a weapon. . . . Right to gut! And from the side, too! That's not an easy target."

"I—I—I—"

"I guess Anders what right about you. Come on."

Crowder walks over the cop, kneels down, turns him onto his back, and starts running his hands over the guy's pockets. He finds a cell phone—"Here we go . . . damn, locked . . . and he has that setting where you can't see the messages without unlocking it."

"C-c-can—"

"No fingerprint sensor. Face unlock or whatever that's called." Crowder turns the guy over. "Fuck. I kind of obliterated that eye. Well that's not gonna work."

He throws the phone into the wall, then he picks it up again and snaps it in half.

"Couldn't one of— of your guys—"

"Maybe. Probably not. But it's not worth getting tracked either way." He searches the dead cop's pockets again and pulls out a badge. "Okay—come on. We gotta get to the van."

I follow Crowder down the hallway but I don't know why. I couldn't tell you why. I couldn't tell you why I shot the cop in the stomach except that he had a gun out and I was holding a gun and something told me he wasn't going to care who I was or that I didn't want to shoot him.

I stop walking. "I— I shot a cop . . ."

Crowder turns around. "Yeah ya did. Don't look so horrified. Cop didn't give a shit about you. None of them do. Cops kill people every day. This is America."

"But— but—"

"Listen—we gotta get to the van, okay? You're gonna hyperventilate—I get it—but we need to get going. Does it suck that we had to kill the guy? Yeah. Okay? I've killed four people today already. None of them were part of the plan. But they had to happen. Shit happens."

"I— I—"

"Hey—look at me. Is your tongue touching the roof of your mouth? Is your *tongue* touching the roof of your *mouth*? Pull it away. Don't let them touch. Got it?"

I do as he says. I peel my tongue from the roof of my mouth. My breathing levels out.

"Got it?"

I nod.

"Good. Can't have a panic attack if your tongue isn't touching the roof of your mouth. Now—come on—we gotta go."

We're not running through the hallway, but we're walking fast. There's a faint echo as we move. I follow Crowder to a door I've not yet seen. Crowder turns the deadbolt. I follow him through it into a large room with a picture window at the front—one of the storefronts. There are shoeboxes and racks of some sort scattered about, but the space is mostly empty. Outside a black van is waiting next to my car.

"Come on. In the van."

I stare at my car. It's just a Ford Fusion, but I have a sort of romantic love for this car. I never had a car in Mexico. This is an American car. My American car. I bought it from one of those lots that had a sign that said, BAD CREDIT? NO PROBLEM. YOU'RE PRE-APPROVED! The thing is, I didn't have bad credit. But the payments were so low, I didn't see how I could have justified going anywhere else.

"Forget it, kid. It's hot. Van's probably hot, too, but we've taken precautions against that. They'll never track it. Those aren't even our plates. One of the guys stole them from a Prius in Sacramento."

The van door opens from the inside. Crowder climbs in. For a moment, I hesitate. My mind is empty, and then it's full of thoughts. This morning I was starting my shift after a night of heavy partying. I was eating a breakfast burrito. I was downing Red Bulls. Now—I have in my body no trace of a hangover. I'm tachycardic. There's a gun in my hand. My life is over, and I'm not sure I ever had any choice in the matter. Somewhere in the course of things I got swept along, and I know—I *know*, deep in the heart of me—that there's no going back. If I get in the van, there's no coming back. I am a hostage; I am not a hostage. Maybe my father would be proud. My mother would be devastated. My *abuela* is somewhere in Mexico City teaching my sister how to be a whore.

"*Come on!*" says Crowder.

I get in the van.

"Had to ice the cop," says Crowder to the driver. "You know where we're going?"

The guy nods.

"Let's get out of here."

The van pulls away. I stare through the tinted windows at my Ford Fusion until I can't see it anymore.

KENNEDY

When we spoke on the phone at Christmas my mother asked me whether I was seeing anyone. She said, "I know you kids out in California are hooking up or whatever all the time, I get it, I don't judge, you have your fun, but is there anyone *special*, Kennedy? Is there anyone in your life right now bringing you joy?"

I answered that talking to her and my father brings me joy.

"That's not what we're asking," said my father.

"Do you have a special someone, anyone at all?" asked my mom.

"We just want to make sure you're happy," my dad said.

I never asked Beckett about his parents. I never thought to ask him about his parents. When Arnold told me Beckett was living off a trust fund, that was the first time it ever occurred to me that maybe Beckett had a father. That's just not how it works out here. Out here, people are entities unto themselves. When you're out here, when you're doing the work we do, you don't have families. You don't have community. I've never met a person on the streets of California and wondered what their children are like, what their home is like. That's just not how people *are* out here. Our existence is separate from elements like that.

One time, after we finished fucking, Beckett told me—

"Hey, lady. I gotta ask you to get outta here."

That's not what Beckett told me. Beckett told me—

"You okay, lady?"

I can't remember what Beckett told me. . . . I blink into the California sun and look around. I am sitting on a planter outside the Comedy Store, the taste of mango and nicotine on my tongue.

"Lady, you okay?"

"I—yeah, I think so."

"I been wonderin' for hours if you were okay. I thought about comin' out to ask ya but you seemed like you were thinkin' real hard."

"How long have I been here?"

"Couple'a' hours. Do you need me to call someone?"

I look at my phone. I've missed at least a dozen calls. There's a calendar notification, 44 minutes old. I'm supposed to be getting into my dress. "Shit," I say. "Sorry, no, no—I don't need you to call anyone. I'm fine."

"Well—listen. I gotta ask you to move along. I gotta get things ready for the Early Show."

I open the Uber app as I stand. "Sorry," I say.

"No worries," says the guy.

As I walk away, he calls out, "Hey, lady. I got a couple'a' comp tickets left. We got Theo Von and Christina P. tonight. You wanna come?"

"I'm sorry? Oh—" I could take a ticket, I tell myself. I could surrender myself to the jokes, the laughter, the joy. But I say, "No, thank you," turning around but not looking up. I stare at the little car on the map. "I have somewhere I need to be."

KEELY

J-Sean is showing the detective a titanium watch band over by the 3D printer, which he has printing *another* mockup of this complicated jewelry design he's been working on ever since I've known him. I can see them through the glass.

I'm in the workshop with Leilani and Maurice. Leilani is just finishing up the new stitching on the dress and it's looking beautiful, at least in this dim light. Maurice is helping her by holding the ruffled section steady with his good, unbandaged hand while she works the machine. He looks pale. He's breathing hard. "Hang in there," I tell him. "I'll give you a blowjob when this is all over."

"So will I," Leilani says. "Hell, we'll do it together. A nice double blowjob. We're lucky the girl's so late. This took way longer than I thought."

"Lucky, I guess," I say, "assuming she ever does show up. Otherwise did we do this whole dress for nothing?"

"I mean, it's fitted for her specifically. And J-Sean doesn't like to reuse complete designs, only themes and inspirations."

Maurice lets out a squeaky wimper.

"Okay—" Leilani says. "Now let's just move the dress back to the table and I just want to go over the back stitch here again by hand, so that it matches this one and this one. You never know with J-Sean, but he might notice if they don't."

"Wear a fucking thimble," I say.

Maurice whimpers again.

"Do you still need his help?"

Leilani, staring at the dress intensely, shakes her head.

"Get out of here," I tell him.

"Could someone take me to the ER?"

"No time. Call an Uber."

Five minutes later and Leilani stands back. She cracks her knuckles. Then she leans back and cracks her spine. For just a moment I get lost in the curvature of her breasts pushing against the soft baseball t-shirt she's wearing. "Okay," she exclaims. "Let's turn the lights up."

I glance through the window and J-Sean is still with the detective by the printer. The detective is staring at her phone, an expression of concern on her face. J-Sean is talking enthusiastically, gesticulating. "Alexa, lights at 80 percent, and white."

Both the brightness and color temperature of the room shift. I stare at the dress.

"Well?"

I nod slowly. "I think . . ."

"Shit," says Leilani.

"What?"

"See this?" She presses down on a tightly ruffled section near the waist and pulls at the fabric. "It's definitely still pink here."

"Hmmm. But it's *in* the fold, right? Like you said before, it kind of looks like a shadow if you don't pull it back like that."

"I don't know . . . I think I want to take a cloth to it with just a little more bleach. Do I have time—"

"Keeeeely!"

I turn. It's J-Sean and he's right in the doorway of the workshop. "H-hey," I manage to stutter. "What's going on."

"Cop lady had to leave. Seemed kinda urgent. She kinda looked super freaked out."

"Oh."

"Yeah, so. You wankers finally finish the alterations?" *Wankers* is a word J-Sean started using occasionally after he started fucking Stewart. "You've been working on them all fuckin— Where's the other guy?"

"Maurice?"

"Yeah, that guy."

"I sent him, um, home," Leilani says. "We're all done. He was getting, um, really hungry. I don't think he'd eaten all day."

"We have vegan snacks over by the wet bar! Lot's of 'em."

"Um—"

"I think Maurice has an eating disorder," I say quickly. "He won't eat anything I offer him."

J-Sean is quiet. "Oh," he finally says. He looks reflective. "Fuck. Well, okay then. Damn—let me know if I can help the guy. Eating disorders are no joke."

"Sure thing," says Leilani. She gives me *a look*.

I give her *a look* back.

"You know, I've been thinkin'—what with people getting murdered and shit—we need to be *kinder* to people, you know? All this social media bullshit. Likes, dislikes, drama—it's all bullshit. People *die* every day. Some people can't even *use* Instagram—because they're *dead*. Fuuuuck that shit."

He pulls out his phone, snaps a selfie, and starts typing. "Dress looks great, ladies," he mutters as he walks out, head staring down at his screen.

"Well—" says Leilani, after he's gone.

"Get this thing ready to put on Thorne," I tell her. "We have to assume she's coming." I leave the workshop and go to get a drink. Something with CBD in it. My watch buzzes. It's not Thorne, but an Instagram notification. J-Sean has posted something. I have notifications turned on for J-Sean's posts because I never know when I'm going to need to reel him in, fix some sort of mess he's made.

I pull out my phone as I reach the wet bar. It's the selfie he just took. The caption starts: *I've been feeling pensive lately . . .*

I get some sparkling water from the SodaStream and add 10 drops of CBD and then after brief consideration add an ounce or so of vodka as well.

I take a sip, and then a gulp, and then I hear Renalda say, in her disgustingly cloying, mild voice, "Hey, Keely? Kennedy Thorne is here."

ESMERALDA

"I think you should drink some juice," I tell Arnold, who does not respond, who lies there in the hospital bed, in this private room, several wires attached to his chest and arm, electrodes against his skin on one end of the wires, a monitor of some sort on the other end. "Arnold, my love, the doctor said you should drink some juice."

The doctor said that Arnold should drink some juice if he wakes up. Then the doctor went away. The doctor said someone would come in to check on Arnold in a little while, and then he went away. He left a bottle of orange juice and said that, if Arnold wakes up, I should get him to drink some juice. He said that the I.V. in his arm on the other side of the bed there was keeping him hydrated and nourished, but that nothing could beat real juice, and that I should get Arnold to drink some if he wakes up—and then he, the doctor, went away.

Arnold has not woken up. The doctor said *if* but when I asked *If?* he corrected himself and said *when. When he wakes up*, the doctor said. *He's just sleeping right now. He's fine. I promise.* This is what the doctor said, and then he went away.

In the ambulance they asked me a bunch of questions I can't remember now—something about what did Arnold take, how much did Arnold take—and that I didn't know the answers to or can't remember knowing the answers to, and they gave him a bunch of pills they said were activated charcoal and said in response to me asking what they were doing that the pills were activated charcoal and that when they got him to the hospital he might need some more charcoal in a liquid form. I couldn't understand why medical professionals would put charcoal into a human's body. I told them, the paramedics, that Arnold had had a very small, very minor stroke once before and a heart attack once before and couldn't this be another one of those? And they said maybe it was a stroke but they didn't think so. They said Arnold took something was what they thought and if they could figure out what it was—if I could help them figure out what it was, if I could remember what it was—they could save him for sure, probably. But I didn't think I knew what it was, so they just gave him a bunch of charcoal and at the hospital they gave him more charcoal and I said to the doctor did they need to pump his stomach and the doctor just stared at me like I was a crazy person. At least that's how I remember it all.

Arnold looks so peaceful, my sweet man. I put my hand on his forehead. "You work so hard," I say. "You work too hard."

Arnold works so hard to take care of his clients. I can see it in his face every day, how much he cares for them, how important to him their success is.

All day, every day, even on the weekends, Arnold is on the phone, sending texts, reading texts, making calls, answering calls. He's calling his clients and he's calling people his clients want to work with and people who want to work with his clients. He's calling directors and producers and even book publishers. Usually he's in his office, at least eight or ten hours a day he's in his office. He drives the Tesla to his office. He likes the Tesla, he says, because it does most of the driving for him, so he can make calls while it's driving. And I know at the office if he's not on the phone he's doing in-person meetings. And if he's not doing meetings he's on his laptop doing emails. Even on the weekends, like today, on a Sunday, when he's not in the office, when he makes a very deliberate point to *not be in the office*, he's making calls and texting and doing emails. He eats bad food. I try to make sure he eats good food, but I'm not stupid, I'm not a dumb wife—I know when I'm not looking he eats bad food. All I can do is make sure he takes his medication and drinks water and gets outside.

Every once in a while, on a Sunday, he'll take the day off. He'll send a text and put an out-of-office message on his email and leave his phone at home and we'll take a drive, the two of us, up the coast or down the coast, stop off somewhere and eat a late breakfast. Not today, of course, because his one client is going to the Oscars. Oh how important that is to Arnold—that his client, *his client!*, is going to the Oscars. We were going to watch the awards together tonight, on the big screen in the screening room, but I don't think we will now. I said, we should have a party, but Arnold didn't want a party. Let's just you and me watch them together, he said. We'll order sushi.

Arnold can eat sushi because it's fish. Fish he can eat. It's red meat he's not supposed to be eating. Or pork. Or sugar.

But the doctor did say if he wakes up, when he wakes up, he should have some juice.

I say, "Arnold, my love, would you like some juice?"

"Nnnnhh," I think I hear him say.

"What's that? Did you say something? Arnold? Would you like some juice?"

But he doesn't make another sound, and I can't be sure he did the first time.

Oh, Arnold. "I remember when we first met . . ." I tell him. "You were so brave." Things weren't going well with his first wife. They were still together, but Arnold assured me he was going to divorce her. He was going to divorce her soon. He did, too, eventually. And then we got married. Poor Arnold. Brave Arnold. His son still won't speak to him and yet every day Arnold wakes up and soldiers on, takes care of his people.

"Have some juice," I tell him.

I open the bottle, insert the straw. I place the straw against his lips.

His lips don't open.

"Oh, Arnold," I say out loud. I place the orange juice back on the little table thing that's attached to the hospital bed. I swing the little table thing out of the way. I lean forward in my chair. I lean way over until my head is on Arnold's chest. I try very carefully to not disturb the wires. I don't know what I'll do if Arnold doesn't wake up. It's been twenty years and without Arnold I just don't know what I'll do.

But then he wakes up, right there beneath me. I feel his chest heave and he says, "Ismi?"

I lift my head and his eyes are open. "Arnold? Arnold!" I'm supposed to do something now but I can't remember what. And then I remember. Yes. "Would you like some juice?" I say. "You're supposed to drink some juice."

"Beckett told me—" Arnold rasps. "Beckett told me that I needed to make sure I watched the Oscars tonight because things were going to be bangin'. That's what he said. He said, 'bangin'. I think it's the Republicans."

And then Arnold is asleep again, just as I grab the juice.

Beckett, I think, is the name of the guy the detective was asking about. What Arnold just said sounds like something I should probably tell the detective. Such a nice woman, that detective. I can't remember her name.

KEELY

J-Sean is staring at Kennedy Thorne, one hand holding his chin, the other hand cradling that arm's elbow. I am holding my breath. Kennedy Thorne is standing on the platform, arms held out at her sides, like she's doing lat raises. I do lat raises every time I work out, those rare times I get to work out. I use ten pound dumbells, up from five a year ago.

Leilani is standing in front of Kennedy Thorne, several heads shorter than her because of the platform. She's making an adjustment near Kennedy's waist. I bet she's holding her breath too. She says, "There," and stands back from the platform, next to me.

"Arms down," J-Sean instructs Kennedy.

Kennedy puts her arms down and J-Sean looks at her for a long time. He takes in the dress's whole front, from the bottom, to the top. I follow his gaze. I am no longer holding my breath—I can't hold my breath that long—but fuck am I breathing slowly. Leilani catches my eye and I give her a shrug, barely perceptible, I hope. J-Sean makes a hmmm sound and walks around the platform, counter-clockwise. When he returns to the front he starts walking around again—clockwise this time. Then he stands in line with Leilani and me, but three times as far from me as I am from Leilani. He says, "Dayyum! That looks fuckin' amazing! Fuck, I do good work." And then he says, to Kennedy, "And, of course, you make it look hot, girl!"

"Thanks," Kennedy says.

I want to high-five Leilani, who retrieves a mirror. Kennedy steps off the platform and stands in front of the mirror. "I love it!"

"Now, darling, what's the plan for your makeup?" J-Sean says. I wasn't going to ask.

"This—this is it. I put some on this morning."

"Right . . . Hmmm . . . Okay. You know what? I love it. Love it! You got like this natural thing going on and it works for you."

"Need anything else?" Leilani asks J-Sean.

"No—I think we're all good here," he says.

"I'm going fucking home, then," she says. "I'm exhausted."

"Hey," J-Sean says, "take tomorrow off."

"Really?"

"Sure thing. I got party stuff tonight. You worked a Sunday. We all worked a Sunday. Have fun. Sleep in. Get drunk."

"Thanks, J-Sean," Leilani says.

"Sure thing." J-Sean turns back to Kennedy Thorne. "Can I, though, just . . . Well—what's your plan for your hair?"

I find Renalda, who is sitting outside, on the ground, back against the brick wall, smoking a cigarette and answering emails on the iPad. "You smoke?" I ask. I'm shocked. I don't touch cigarettes—unless I'm offered one at a party or something.

She looks up at me. "Shit," she says. This is the first time I've heard her swear. She stands quickly, throwing the cigarette to the ground and stamping it out with her shoe. "What's up?" she asks, as if I never saw the cigarette, as if she somehow believes I never saw the cigarette.

I tell her she can head home whenever she feels like she's finished up, and that everyone's taking the day off tomorrow, and she should too.

"Oh—hey—thanks!" she says.

"No problem," I tell her. I'm about to go back inside, but then I ask her, "Hey—you . . . I dunno . . . doing okay? With . . . all this?"

"Oh—yeah," she says. "Of course!"

"Okay," I say.

"Thanks," she says.

"No problem."

A black Lincoln Town Car has just pulled up to the curb.

Back inside, J-Sean and Kennedy Thorne are standing by the wet bar. Kennedy is laughing at something J-Sean has said. This is unusual. It's almost unsettling. I can't remember the last time I heard J-Sean make a joke. "I think your car is here," I tell her.

"Oh, gosh—" she says. "Would you believe I've never been in a limo before?"

"Nervous?" J-Sean asks.

"A little bit. This movie was the biggest thing I've ever done."

"I actually saw it," J-Sean says. "I loved it."

"Wow—really?"

This is the first I've heard him mention it.

"Yeah! I love Ryan Gosling. There's no way I couldn't have seen it."

"Oh . . ." Kennedy says. "That's not— I mean, I was in that one, but that's just up for Best Screenplay. I didn't write it. But I was also in *In My Eyes, Your Heart*, which is up for Best Picture."

"Ah. I didn't see that one."

"I had a scene with George Clooney."

J-Sean shrugs.

"Anyway," Kennedy says, "I guess I should get going. Do you know where my bag is?"

I retrieve her blood-red suede purse from the chair on which Renalda placed it. I hand it to her. "That doesn't exactly go with the dress," I point out.

"I think they have somewhere I can put it. At the theater."

"Okay." I don't think they do.

She heads to the door, holding the hem of the dress off the floor.

"Hey—" J-Sean calls after her.

She turns back.

"I, uh," he says. "I just wanted to say . . . well, you know— we're cool. No hard feelings and shit. 'S' all good."

"Um . . . okay."

"I'm just tryin' to be more compassionate, y'know? So, yeah, sorry for being so pissed off about everything."

"It's . . . okay?"

"J-Sean," I say. "I think she's running late."

"Right, right. Cool. Okay, cool. Have a good time. Maybe we'll see you at one of the after parties."

When she's gone, I want to say something to J-Sean, but I don't know what. Then his phone rings. He answers and I can tell by the way he says "Hey, babe" that it's Stuart. And I can tell by the look on his face that Stuart is already high. J-Sean takes the call upstairs, and I survey the studio.

There are a couple dirty glasses and half-full coffee mug on the wet bar. I place them in the sink and then wipe a coffee stain from the bar's surface. I push the mirror against a wall. I pick up the platform Kennedy Thorne was standing on and carry it over to the side of the studio, set it down next to the mirror. I return to the dress mannequin and wheel it into the workshop. The workshop is a little untidy but it can wait until tomorrow. There's a splatter of dried blood on the drafting table. I take a paper towel and wet it with my tongue and wipe at the blood and it comes off, with effort. I throw the towel away. I tell Alexa to turn off the workshop lights. Back in the studio Renalda is pulling a messenger back over her shoulder near the door. She smiles at me and waves before she leaves. I raise my hand to her.

Alone now, I sit in a chair. I just sit.

After some time, J-Sean comes back down.

"Stuart okay?" I ask.

"Stuart's fucking fucked up. But it's whatever. I think I'm going to break up with him. I mean, like, eventually." He looks at me. "Let's find you someting to wear."

KENNEDY

I told J-Sean Laurentius and his assistant or partner or whatever she is that I've never been in a limo before. That wasn't true. I once took a limo to a fundraiser with a Democratic presidential candidate who I won't name. His name doesn't matter. You probably wouldn't even know it, his name. This was like two years ago and he dropped out of the race before the first debate. He said he was going to change America. He said he was going to bring us together—us meaning *all of us*, I assume. Somehow I ended up in his limo. I was a little high, so I don't remember how I ended up in his limo. This was one of the first gigs I did when I moved to L.A. It might have been the first public thing Arnold arranged for me as my agent. I do remember asking Arnold why this event, why a political event, when I was trying to be an actress and a social media star. And he said something like, because this guy needs to appeal to young people, young people like you and your followers. Something else like, people care what you have to say, after that thing you said about Trump. I was at like a couple hundred thousand followers at the time, maybe. I was a little high. I don't do drugs, I don't smoke marijuana anymore,

I don't think pot should be legalized—but sometimes I do get a little high. You understand, don't you? Sometimes I just get a little high, when I don't think anybody will know about it. The Democratic presidential candidate tried to kiss me in his limo. This—the Democratic presidential candidate's limo—is another memory I have, although I think for a time there I forgot it.

Nobody is trying to kiss me in *this* limo. I'm alone in *this* limo. The driver was very kind and welcomed me and said he hoped I was having a good day, and he told me there was vodka in the little bar back here, and then he raised the privacy screen.

I'm drinking the vodka, just a finger's worth, so it doesn't count. There's no lime back here. There is club soda, but I haven't added it to the vodka. I sip the vodka on its own.

On its own . . .

On its own what? What is it that belongs solely to this clear, sharp alcoholic beverage?

On its own. On my own now.

The crystalline glass of vodka is in one hand. My phone is in the other. I unlock my phone. There are hundreds of comments on my photo from this morning of the CBD cold brew. There's a private message from the account of the CBD cold brew company:

Hey, Kennedy! Love the photo! Glad to hear you love our product. We'd be happy to send you some more! DM me your address and I'll get a case sent out to you ASAP. Heart emoji. Heart emoji. Heart emoji. Signed: someone from their fucking marketing team.

I type back thank you. I type out Arnold's phone number —the only number I know by heart—and email address—the only email address I know by heart. I tell the person from their fucking marketing team to speak to Arnold. He'll arrange everything.

There are some comments on a post about Beckett. Rumors floating around that I was sleeping with Beckett Shaw. Rumors floating around that I was dating Beckett Shaw. Rumors floating around that I was engaged to Beckett Shaw. So many condolences. So many judgements. Beckett deserved better than me, I'm told. Someone hopes I die, too.

I haven't heard from Arnold since our late breakfast. I'm feeling a little hungry. I'm worried about Arnold. He needs to take it easier, I think, although I've never told him I feel that way.

"Everything okay back there?" a voice says. It sounds far away.

I realize it's the driver. I press the button next to the privacy screen. "Yes, thank you." After a moment I ask, "You?"

"Slight detour up ahead," he says. "They've closed North Highland for some reason. Should be there in just a few minutes though."

"Thanks," I say.

I look out the tinted window to my right. This is Hollywood. This place is Hollywood. This night is Hollywood. I am part of this.

In my hand, my phone vibrates.

Hey, love, my mom has texted. *We watched the movie again last night. We're watching the ceremony tonight. Nanna is here. I even made canapes. Good luck!*

I can't think of what to say, so I put my phone on Do Not Disturb.

I go to put my phone away, but then I pause. I open Youtube. I run a search. I tap a thumbnail from long ago:

Hey guys what's up it's Beckett back with another video

CARLOS

I've been told that in the old days taxi drivers had to know the city in which they drove—sometimes even adjacent cities, towns, and suburbs. There are apps that tell me where to go when I drive. So I don't know what street we're on right now, only that we're a few blocks over from Hollywood Boulevard, a few blocks over from the Dolby Theatre. I know it's the Dolby Theatre we're a few blocks over from only because Anders said it was the Dolby Theatre. He said this back at what I've come to think of in just a few short hours as headquarters. He said, "Let's go over the layout again" and pulled a map up on his projector.

Now he says, "Let's go over the plan again, briefly, one last time."

We're in the parking garage of a high-rise apartment building, both vans, eight people. The rest of the guys who were at the headquarters aren't here. They've gone somewhere else. I don't know where. I guess they're just not part of this part of the plan.

When we pulled into the parking garage I asked, "Isn't someone going to catch us here? Isn't it suspicious, a white van and a black van down here like this? Cavorting?" I did not know until that moment that I knew the word *cavorting*.

"Nah," Crowder said. "Billy lives in these apartments. Both vans are registered to him, here, in the building."

The guy in the front seat, the one driving the van, whose name I learned on the way here is Marko, said, "It's a big sacrifice he's making, Billy, because they got cameras down here and shit, so once we follow through they're going to come here, looking for him."

"Yeah," Crowder said, "but by then it won't matter."

"Sure won't," the driver said.

The doors of both vans are open and all us guys are sitting so that we can see and hear Anders, who's standing between them, the only one not in a van. "One last time," Crowder says.

It's a simple plan: Crowder, myself, and Marko in our van, Marko driving. Several other guys in the other van. I still can't remember everyone's names. The drivers . . . well, I'm sure you can imagine what the plan is, right? The drivers take the vans down Hollywood Boulevard, through the barricades, through the people. That's part one. Part two is . . . well . . .

"You sure you up for this, kid?" Anders says to me. It's not like any of these guys are much older than me—Anders and Crowder are maybe 30—but they all—the ones who talk to me —call me kid.

I nod.

"It's not too late to back out. It's a big thing you're doing. I could still shuffle some guys around."

"I'm good," I croak. Because I'm not stupid. I know there's no coming back from this day. If I said I wanted out,

Anders would have Crowder take me behind a car and shoot me or snap my neck and leave me in a stairwell or a dumpster. And if I follow through with the current circumstances, I'm dead too. My job is to push a button. Crowder's job is to push the button if I don't push the button. They say the button triggers a device that's already been placed in the Dolby Theatre, but I know that can't be true. The device is in the locked case in the back of the van. I saw Crowder unlock the case and inspect its contents, fiddle with them. Even now from where I'm sitting I can see that the other van has a similar case inside it. The only thing I don't understand is why so many of us? Three guys in this van, three guys in the other van. Why can't the drivers do it all? Why two vans? Why do so many of us have to die?

"Good man," Anders says. "You're really comin' through for us today. It means more than you could know." Then his voice changes. It doesn't get louder, but clearer, bolder. "That goes for all of you," he says. "You're noble men. The world has nearly run out of noble men, but we are noble men. Men who stand up, who do what must be done. A thousand years ago, a hundred years ago, the world was full of men who were warriors. America was full of warriors. We're the only warriors left now, at least in the Failling West. Did you know the first red carpet was rolled out twenty-five hundred years ago? It's true. Aeschylus wrote about it. Agamemnon returned from the Trojan war and his wife rolled out a red carpet for him. She told him the foot of a warrior like him should not touch the Earth after such a glorious battle. And you know what he said? Do you? He said, 'I am a mortal, a man; I cannot trample upon these tinted splendors without fear thrown in my path.' If only men, not to mention women, today had such humility—then we would not need to do what we are about to do."

And now Anders surprises me: he bows his head, silently. The other men bow their heads. I have not prayed since I left Mexico. I find myself bowing my head, too.

"Okay," Anders says after a minute or two. He shakes each of our hands. "Good luck," he says, nodding at us in turn. "Oh, and let's change the plates again before you head out." And then he walks away.

When the van door is closed, I ask, "Anders isn't coming with us?"

"Of course not," Crowder says. "Our army needs him. He has to lead the next strike. And the next. And the next."

ADELINE

Paul is dead and there is red in front of my eyes. My hands grip the steering wheel and I'm afraid they'll never come off. There's a second forensics team at an abandoned shopping mall in El Segundo. I have abandoned the forensics team at the abandoned shopping mall. There is an APB out on two vans— a black van and a white van—and their license plate numbers. There is a dead cop in an abandoned shopping mall in El Segundo.

When you meditate, if you meditate long enough and for enough days, you eventually come to the realization that you are in control of nothing. Everything that happens is happening to you. You are just an observer, not a participant. This realization first happened to me long ago, on retreat in Northern Oregon. The thing about this realization is that it is not a permanent one. It comes all at once and then disappears, for you cannot live your life that way—not until you are ready. If you are lucky, the realization comes again, and again, and maybe someday it stays, because you are ready now. This realization first happened to me on retreat in Northern Oregon a decade ago. It happened again when my child was born. And again when my wife took her final breaths. It's happening now. *I* am not driving this car.

Detective Paul Gump was an asshole, but he did not deserve to die. When the day is over I will have to be the one to tell his wife and child.

The radio on my dashboard crackles to life. "Detective Ramos, come in. Detective Ramos, come in."

I pick up the transmitter. "This is Ramos. Hi, Lieutenant."

"Adeline? What the hell is going on? They told me you showed up to the scene and then just stormed off. Drove off. Where are you going?"

"The Oscars."

"What the—? Did I hear you right? The Academy Awards?"

"There's a witness there I need to talk to."

"A witness? At the Oscars? Paul's killer? Shaw's killer?"

"Don't know. Doubt it. But I need to talk to her. Now."

"Adeline—we just got a call in about the Oscars. From one of your other witnesses. It sounded like a threat. Or the threat of a threat."

"What did they say?"

"Not much. Just that Beckett Shaw said something about a bang."

"What else?"

"We got an anonymous tip on the Shaw livestream from this morning. It's . . . hard to decipher. There might be some legitimacy to the threat."

"Call in an evacuation notice. Get everyone off the red carpet."

"It's not that simple. Security is private. We don't even know who to route the order through."

I consider my options. The way I see it, I have only one.

"Fine," I say. "*I'll* do it."

"*What? Adeline!*"

"I said I'll do it."

I turn the radio off.

CARLOS

"You ready, kid?" Crowder asks.

Marko drives the van. I hold the small black remote control in my hand. What I'm supposed to do is flip the switch —the safety—and then press the button.

"I'm not a kid," I snap.

Crowder holds up his hands. One has his gun in it. "Whoa. My bad. Sorry."

"Almost there," Marko says. "Remember—wait until we've achieved maximum penetration. Anders says the signal will be strongest that way."

The signal, I think, and laugh.

KENNEDY

Another memory I have is of my Nanna's kitchen. I'm nine years old and we're baking sourdough bread and canning jars of marmalade.

Nanna is saying, "You can make marmalade from any kind of citrus fruit. Oranges. Grapefruits. Lemons. You name it. Most people make it from bitter oranges. But my favorite marmalades are those made from bergamots or blood oranges. Or both."

Today we're making marmalade from blood oranges.

I ask my Nanna what the difference is between marmalade and jam.

"The peel," she says. "Marmalade is made with the peel, which is why we only use oranges and citrus fruit like that. Berries don't have peels."

Then Nanna tells me about the sourdough, about fermentation.

I ask Nanna whether Mom and Dad are going to be okay.

"Of course they are," she reassures me. "They're just having a bit of a disagreement today. But everyone has disagreements sometimes. Even people who love each other very very much."

In the pot on the stove, the marmalade is deep red, the color of the carpet on which I'm standing now, nearly two decades later.

I'm walking down the carpet, down the press line because the movie I'm in is a nominee, looking at the hem of my dress, which covers my shoes. Everyone is here with someone. I never thought to bring a plus-one. I had every right to bring a plus-one, but I never thought to invite someone. Not Arnold, not my mom, not Beckett. I could tell Beckett was angry that he wasn't invited, but it didn't occur to me, not until right this very second, that it was because *I* didn't invite him that he was angry.

If I'd invited him, would he have come? If I'd invited him, would he *be here*?

I don't know. I never will.

So I raise my head. There are people all around me. Famous people. Actors and directors and musicians and reporters. Lady Gaga is wearing what I think is supposed to be a human-size form-fitting traffic cone, but it kind of looks like she threw it together at the last minute. It might be a candy corn. John Legend's skin glows from beneath a tasteful dark blue tuxedo with silver trim. He's up for both Best Supporting Actor and Best Song this year.

Everything around me is lights and people. It's all gold and red and buttery cream. Silks and sequins and velvet. "Over here"s and "You look wonderful this evening"s. Flashbulbs and cameras and microphones. Jennifer Lawrence is standing next to Bradley Cooper, posing for a photograph. They're up for Best Actress and Actor—again—for the same movie.

I hold my phone out in front of me, turn it around to the selfie cam, and post a ten-second video to my Story. I say something to my followers about being excited, about being grateful. Then I put the phone away. It turns out there was nowhere to put my bag—also turns out Arnold got me the limo only for the ride here, not the ride home—so I hold it in front of me, close to my body, conscious of the fact that it doesn't match my dress. I promise myself I won't pull my phone out again tonight.

I know no one here, not personally. Not enough to talk to them.

But then I spot George Clooney a dozen feet away, wearing a black tuxedo and a black tie, standing with his wife, talking to a blonde woman with a microphone, a cameraman behind her. And though he and I have never spoken more than a few words, I know that if someone here remembers me, it'll be him.

Before I can get to him, a microphone is in *my* face. Another blonde woman. Another bearded cameraman behind her. The microphone says *Entertainment Tonight* or *Access Hollywood* or *Good Morning America* or one of those. I try to read it, to make out which one it says, but I'm being honest when I say it doesn't matter, they all look the same.

The woman says, "Look who it is! It's Kennedy Thorne. Popular Instagram influencer and budding actress. Miss Thorne, it's so great to see you on the red carpet! This is your first time, right? What do you think?"

The microphone hovers in front of my mouth. So I say, "Thank you. It's great to be here."

"This is a J-Sean Laurentius, isn't it?"

At first I don't know what she's talking about, referring to a thing as a person, but then I realize she means the dress.

"Yes, it is," I say.

"Why don't you tell us a bit about it?"

"Well—I—it's—" I don't know anything about the dress. The bag in my hand feels so out of place. I wait for the woman to tell me how out of place it is.

"I understand this is the first dress J-Sean has designed for an Oscars attendee—is that right?"

"Yes, yes," I say, not knowing whether that's the case.

The woman looks at her cameraman's camera. "J-Sean Laurentius, you all may remember, designed the very stylish numbers Lady Gaga and Miley Cyrus each wore to the VMAs last year, but this is the first time one of the acclaimed up-and-coming designer's pieces has been seen here at the Academy Awards." She turns back to me. "Why you, Miss Thorne?"

"Why—what?"

"Why do you think J-Sean chose you as the first person to represent his brand at this prestigious show?"

"I think my agent bribed him," I say.

She laughs. "Oh my—well, lucky you then, I suppose. Anyway, I think J-Sean did it because he knows what a great actress you are, what a star you're going to be. Speaking of stars, we have so many stars to get to here on the Red Carpet, so let's see who else we can find. Back to you, Robin!"

Before I can say anything else, she's gone, and I'm alone again. But George spots me now, and behind him is Lupita Nyong'o, who was also in *In My Eyes, Your Heart* but who I didn't have any scenes with and who wasn't even on set the day I was. George says something to Lupita and waves. Together they start walking toward me, George's wife following behind.

Then a man behind me says my name, so I turn around. I don't know for sure, but I think it's Steven Spielberg. He tells me he enjoyed my performance—and that we should talk later because he's working on something—a miniseries for a streaming service—he thinks I might be perfect in.

Right before George and Lupita get to me there's another microphone in front of my mouth, and I'm being asked something about my dress again. Something else about J-Sean Laurentius. And then what was it like to work with George Clooney. I know that, right now, this year, anyone who cares about me cares only to the extent that they can define me by my association with somebody else. By the clothes I'm wearing, or the star I flirted with, or the politician whose campaign I advocated for. But as someone calls out my name from across the Carpet, and as a sound like a gunshot goes off from one side of the golden crowd, and as a deafening crash sounds from across the other, I am certain of one thing: It won't always be this way. I'm an up-and-coming star. The blonde woman said so herself. Soon, everyone will know me for me, for who the fuck *I* am.

And I will have everything I ever wanted.

ABOUT THE AUTHOR

Shawn Mihalik is the author of six books. He's deeply interested in many things. Shawn lives in Central Oregon with his wife and two cats.